GRANNY GOES VIRAL

A SECRET AGENT GRANNY MYSTERY BOOK 11

HARPER LIN

ONE

I've faced my fair share of villains in my life—terrorists, double agents, arms dealers—but none were quite as terrifying as the sea of ring lights and selfie sticks currently surrounding me. Bryce Thornton, Cheerville's golden boy and self-proclaimed social media king, was hosting his charity auction in the town's modest community center, and somehow, I'd been roped into attending.

Bryce, at the tender age of twenty-six, had a jawline sharper than a CIA-issued knife and a following that stretched from Cheerville to the farthest corners of TikTok. With his perfectly styled hair, meticulously curated wardrobe, and just the right amount of swagger, he was the kind of man who made moms swoon, young women sigh, and teenage girls shriek. Even some of the men seemed unable to resist his charm. Personally, I found him exhausting.

"Barbara, isn't this exciting?" Pauline whispered, clutching my arm. She was positively glowing, her cheeks flushed as though she'd just walked through a romantic fantasy novel instead of a community center gymnasium repurposed for influencer chaos.

"Exciting? No. Loud? Yes," I muttered, shifting uncomfortably in my chair. My companions, however, were oblivious.

Pauline, though older, had the starry-eyed enthusiasm of a teenager. Gretchen, seated to her right, nodded along as she adjusted her walker to a more convenient position. Plump and eternally optimistic, Gretchen was the kind of person who could find the silver lining in a hailstorm.

"I hope there's champagne," Gretchen said. "I didn't skip my nap for sparkling water."

As the spectacle unfolded before me, I couldn't help but reflect on how far my life had strayed from its original trajectory. It was enough to make me laugh. Almost.

I'm Barbara Gold. Age: 71. Height: 5'5". Eyes:

blue. Hair: gray. Weight: classified. Specialties: undercover surveillance, small arms, chemical weapons, Middle Eastern and Latin American politics. Current status: Retired CIA agent, widow, and grandmother.

I never intended for my retirement to be filled with intrigue, but trouble has a way of finding me. And in a town like Cheerville, the line between normalcy and chaos is paper-thin.

Tonight's chaos was named Bryce Thornton.

The gymnasium had been transformed into a high-tech spectacle. Rows of auction items were laid out under strategic lighting: designer handbags, exclusive spa packages, and as a centrepiece, a sleek smartwatch on a rotating pedestal. The scent of expensive cologne and catered hors d'oeuvres mingled in the air, adding to the surreal juxtaposition of opulence in a space better suited for high school basketball games.

"There he is!" Pauline whispered, practically vibrating with excitement as she pointed toward the center of the room.

Bryce Thornton stood like a human sun, drawing the entire room into his orbit. He wore slim-fit trousers, an impeccably tailored white shirt, and a blazer that made "casual" look expensive. Every movement was precise yet effortless, as though choreographed by some invisible PR team. His hair was styled to perfection, his teeth dazzling under the lights. The crowd leaned toward him like plants reaching for sunlight.

"Do you think he knows how attractive he is?" Gretchen asked, craning her neck for a better view.

"Oh, he knows," I said dryly. "That kind of confidence isn't accidental."

Bryce was surrounded by fans, mostly women, though a few men lingered nearby, trying to adopt his signature look of suave indifference. Phones hovered in the air, capturing every angle of the man who, by his own admission, was "redefining what it means to give back." I resisted the urge to roll my eyes.

"He's a genius," Gretchen said, clapping her hands together with such enthusiasm that her walker wobbled slightly. "Turning his fame into philanthropy? What a role model!"

"Philanthropy," I repeated, watching Bryce pose for a picture with two women old enough to be his mother. He leaned in just enough to seem charming but not so close as to disturb his immaculate hair.

"Nothing screams selflessness like filming it for millions of strangers."

"Barbara, you're such a cynic," Gretchen said, but her tone was indulgent rather than critical. She was too busy smiling at Bryce's every move, her plump cheeks glowing with delight.

Gretchen's good nature made it difficult to indulge fully in my sarcasm. These outings weren't really my scene—too many people, too much noise—but with Liz off honeymooning with her new husband, I had resolved to make more of an effort with Pauline and Gretchen. They were good people I met in book club, and I wanted to get to know them better. Even if that meant enduring Bryce Thornton's endless row of perfect teeth and carefully rehearsed humility.

Before I could sharpen my wit any further, Octavian appeared at my side, holding two drinks. His timing, as always, was impeccable. His smile was warm, his eyes sparkling with humor as they took in the spectacle around us.

Octavian, brushing a quick kiss on my cheek, said, "Don't knock Bryce. He might surprise you."

"He's about as surprising as a pop-up ad," I said, accepting the glass he handed me with a nod of thanks. I swirled the liquid and took a cautious sip, grimacing. "I think this is the champagne Gretchen was hoping for. But it's pretending to be apple juice."

Octavian chuckled. "Sounds like they didn't splurge on the good stuff. What's a charity auction without a budget for decent wine and alcohol?"

"Yes. Budget-friendly and Bryce Thornton don't belong in the same sentence," I said. "Even if this wine probably comes with a hashtag."

Octavian had a knack for softening my sharper edges, a quality I both appreciated and found mildly irritating at times. His optimism had a way of balancing out my skepticism, especially on evenings like this one. Even he, however, couldn't convince me that Bryce Thornton was anything other than a spectacle—a carefully curated performance designed to dazzle and exhaust in equal measure.

Bryce raised his hand, silencing the chatter as he stepped to the center of the stage. "Ladies and gentlemen, and all my fans watching from home," he began, gesturing to a crew live-streaming the event. The ring lights around the phones lit his face like a halo, emphasizing his already perfect cheekbones. His voice was smooth and confident, carrying easily over the crowd. "Tonight, we're here to make a difference—and to have some fun while we're at it!"

A ripple of applause echoed through the room.

Pauline clapped so enthusiastically that I feared she might dislocate something. Gretchen, seated to her right, gave a little whoop, which earned her a few glances. She responded by grinning widely and waving to no one in particular.

Bryce launched into his speech, seamlessly shifting into the role of motivational guru. He extolled the virtues of community and charity, sprinkling in just enough personal anecdotes to keep his audience hooked. The lighting team even dimmed the overheads slightly, casting an intimate glow over the stage.

"Growing up, I didn't have much," he said, his voice dropping into a humble register that practically begged for sympathy. "But I had a dream—and the drive to chase it."

"Did he mention the part where his parents bought him a startup?" I muttered to Octavian, keeping my voice low. Octavian smothered a laugh behind his wine glass, his shoulders shaking with amusement.

"Shh," Pauline hissed, fixing me with a stern look. "This is important."

Bryce, oblivious to my commentary, paused dramatically, letting the weight of his words settle over the room. "I realized early on that success isn't just about what you achieve for yourself. It's about what you give back."

The crowd murmured in agreement, heads nodding as though he'd just solved world hunger. Bryce gestured toward the rotating pedestal displaying the sleek smartwatch at the center of the auction. The spotlight caught the watch's face, making it gleam like a treasure in a pirate's hoard.

"This," Bryce said, lifting the watch with the reverence of a priest holding a sacred relic, "isn't just a smartwatch. It's a statement. A symbol of what's possible when innovation meets generosity. And tonight, all proceeds from this auction will go toward building a brighter future."

Another round of applause erupted, louder this time. Pauline looked on the verge of tears, dabbing her eyes with a napkin, while Gretchen gave a thumbs-up in Bryce's direction as though he could see her from across the room.

"He's really working the crowd," Octavian murmured, his tone both amused and impressed.

"Oh, he's a master," I said dryly, taking another sip of my apple-juice masquerading as champagne. "If only that watch could also cure gullibility."

Bryce turned to the camera crew, his smile broad and gleaming. "And to everyone watching from home—don't forget, you can participate in the auction online! The link is in my bio. Together, we can make a difference."

The room was practically vibrating with energy as Bryce continued his speech, weaving a tale of triumph and perseverance that would have made even the most hardened skeptic nod along. But not me. My attention was already drifting to the smartwatch itself, its sleek design and faint glow stirring something in the back of my mind—a sense that there was more to it than met the eye.

The auction officially began, with Bryce narrating. He weaved just enough humor and personal anecdotes into his descriptions to keep the crowd hanging on his every word. A designer handbag fetched $2,000 after a spirited bidding war between two women in the front row. A spa retreat went for $5,000, the winner waving her paddle with the air of someone who'd just won the lottery. The bids came fast and furious, the room buzzing with energy.

Octavian leaned in slightly, murmuring, "You've got to hand it to him—he's good at this."

"He's something," I replied, though my tone was less admiring. My attention was drawn to the periphery of the room, where the enthusiasm wasn't quite as uniform.

I noticed a pair standing near the side of the room. The woman was striking, with flowing red hair, a sharp outfit that looked effortless, and the kind of poise that screamed "influencer." She radiated the confidence of someone used to being in front of a camera, unlike the man standing with her. He was Bryce's age but lacked his effortless charm. While Bryce lit up the room with charisma, this man seemed to blend into the shadows.

The two were in deep conversation, their heads tilted slightly toward one another. Whatever they were discussing, it wasn't the spa retreats or handbags being auctioned off. The man's posture was rigid, his body angled slightly away from her as if guarding against eavesdroppers. The woman, on the other hand, leaned in closer, her expression shifting between exasperation and urgency.

I sipped my champagne, letting my gaze linger on them without making it obvious. "Who's that?" I asked Octavian, nodding subtly toward the pair.

Octavian followed my line of sight, his brow furrowing slightly. "The woman looks like Fiona Younger," he said. "You know, the influencer. Bryce's friend. She's been around Cheerville lately, shooting content or whatever it is they call it."

"And the man?" I asked, keeping my tone casual.

"Don't recognize him," Octavian admitted, leaning back in his chair.

"Is it just me," I said, "or does it feel like there's more going on here than overpriced handbags?"

"You're always looking for a conspiracy," he replied, though his tone was light. He took a sip of his wine, glancing around the room with casual curiosity. "Maybe you should relax and enjoy yourself for once."

"Relaxation is for people who don't have instincts," I murmured.

Octavian chuckled softly, but his gaze followed mine toward the duo again. He tilted his head slightly, a flicker of curiosity crossing his face.

Bryce continued to dazzle the crowd. He gestured toward the rotating pedestal, where the watch gleamed under the lights like the crown jewel of the evening. "This, my friends, is the future," he said, his voice ringing with certainty. He lifted the sleek device for all to see, tilting it slightly so the light caught its polished surface. "Cutting-edge technology meets everyday convenience. It's not just a watch; it's a statement. And tonight, it could be yours."

The room erupted into applause, though I

noticed that not everyone was clapping. The man next to Fiona frowned and crossed his arms.

Bryce took the smartwatch off the pedestal. "This is the pinnacle of innovation. Imagine a device that not only keeps you connected but enhances your life in ways you've never imagined."

The crowd leaned forward, captivated. Cameras flashed in a frenzy, the light reflecting off the polished surface of the smartwatch like a miniature spotlight. I caught Gretchen mouthing, "Amazing," her eyes wide with admiration.

Bryce strapped the watch onto his wrist, his smile widening as though he were the inventor of time itself. "Let me show you how it works," he said, his voice dipping into that irresistible tone influencers used to make every gadget seem indispensable. He pressed a button on the side.

"Stylish, functional, and completely revolutionary," Bryce declared, holding up his wrist like a model in a high-end jewelry ad. The crowd murmured in approval, the kind of awe reserved for fireworks displays and life-changing infomercials.

Then it happened.

At first, it was subtle—a slight falter in his step, a momentary flicker in his confident expression. But then his eyes widened, and he clutched his chest as though an invisible force had gripped him. Bryce staggered backward, his face draining of color.

"Someone... call..." he rasped, his voice barely audible. His knees buckled, and he crumpled to the stage.

For a second, the room froze in collective disbelief. Then chaos erupted.

Fans screamed, their shrill voices slicing through the silence like sirens. Phones shot into the air, not to help but to capture every angle of Bryce's collapse. The camera crew surged forward, their lenses trained on him like vultures circling fresh prey.

Pauline let out a gasp so loud it could have been part of the soundtrack. Gretchen fanned Pauline with a brochure to prevent her from fainting. Chairs rattled as people scrambled to get closer or farther away, unsure whether to help or flee.

I stood rooted in place, my mind racing. The scene unfolded around me like a slow-motion disaster, but my focus was razor-sharp. While everyone else panicked, I saw that Bryce's lips were faintly blue, his fingers twitching in a rhythmic pattern I recognized all too well.

Poison.

And not just any poison.

This was deliberate, targeted, and executed with

precision. Someone had killed Bryce Thornton, and they'd done it in front of an audience of thousands.

I felt Octavian's hand on my arm, his voice steady but concerned. "Barbara. What are you thinking?"

"That this wasn't an accident," I said quietly, my gaze fixed on Bryce's motionless form. "This was murder."

TWO

By the time the police arrived, the community center was a scene of chaos, filled with flashing lights and speculative whispers. Red-and-blue strobes from the patrol cars painted the gymnasium walls in a surreal, almost garish glow. Most of the guests had fled, clutching their designer handbags and phones, but a few lingered in uneasy clusters. Their voices were low, their words fragmented, as if sharing their theories in hushed tones would somehow protect them from what they'd witnessed.

Bryce Thornton's body had been wheeled away minutes earlier, covered in a sterile white sheet, his megawatt smile extinguished. During the initial examination, one of the paramedics had removed the smartwatch from his wrist. I noticed the brief pause as the paramedic turned the device over in his gloved hand, his gaze lingering on it for a moment, before they gave it to one of the officers and continued their work.

The officer bagged it as evidence with all the care of someone handling a mildly interesting trinket. The rookie's expression betrayed his inexperience; he seemed unsure whether the watch was significant or just another piece of technology. Either way, the officer moved on quickly, distracted by the task of questioning two women. The watch, now sealed in its evidence bag, sat on a table, its gleaming surface catching the spotlight like a forgotten trophy.

The police bustled about, taking statements and jotting notes, their movements efficient but perfunctory. Most of the guests seemed too rattled to be helpful, their accounts littered with inconsistencies and hyperbole. Still, murmurs of "poison" and "sabotage" rippled through the room like a quiet rebellion against the official narrative.

Chief Grimal, Cheerville's very own immovable object, stood at the center of it all. His face was set in his usual expression of mild annoyance, but there was an extra edge to his voice as he addressed the crowd.

"Heart attack," he announced, loud enough for

everyone to hear. "Happens all the time. Nothing suspicious here, folks. Until you saw something unusual you'd like to share, go home and get some rest."

The statement landed like a gavel, silencing most of the murmurs but not the unease. A collective ripple of dissatisfaction spread through the room, especially from the older attendees, who knew enough about life and death to spot the signs of something unnatural.

Gretchen, never one to stay silent when she disagreed, shook her head emphatically. The tennis balls on her walker slid against the floor as she shifted her weight, her face a picture of indignation. "Didn't they see his lips?" she muttered, her voice low but insistent. "They were blue! Heart attacks don't do that."

Pauline clutched Gretchen's arm for balance. "And he said something," she added, her voice trembling. "He tried to call for help. Does a heart attack give you time for that?"

Chief Grimal's gaze swept over the two women, his patience clearly wearing thin. "You're reading too much into this," he said brusquely. "Stick to your hobbies. Let the professionals handle it."

The dismissal stung, and I saw Gretchen's lips

tighten in irritation. Pauline looked away, clutching her handbag as though it might steady her nerves. Grimal didn't give either of them a chance to reply; his attention was already shifting to another officer motioning him toward the far end of the room.

From the corner of my eye, I caught movement near the exit. A man who was with Fiona Younger earlier was speaking briefly to an officer, his gestures precise but restrained, as though measuring every word. His face was calm, but his eyes darted occasionally to the now-empty stage where Bryce had collapsed. Moments later, the officer waved him off, and the man disappeared into the night.

Something about him raised my hackles. I didn't know his name yet, but I intended to.

Gretchen patted Pauline's arm. "Come on, let's get out of here. You need tea, and I need to put my feet up."

Pauline nodded weakly, letting Gretchen guide her toward the exit. She turned back to me and Octavian. "Are you coming?"

"You go ahead without us," I said, waving them off with a reassuring smile.

They didn't think twice, their focus entirely on getting home. As they walked away, I felt Octavian's gaze settle on me.

"So, what are you going to do?" he asked, his voice low.

I glanced at him, pretending not to understand. "Do?"

"Barbara," he said, tilting his head. "I know that look. You're already figuring out your next move."

"Don't be ridiculous," I replied lightly, though I didn't bother trying to convince him.

"Right," he said with a wry smile. "You just happen to be the last one here, watching the police like you're grading their performance."

I shrugged, my attention flicking back to the scene. The smartwatch was in an evidence bag sitting on a table. They'd take it away soon. My chest tightened. It wasn't just a device—it was the key. Whatever had happened to Bryce, the answers were locked inside that innocuous piece of tech.

"You're going to poke around," Octavian said, his voice carrying a mix of concern and resignation. "You can't help yourself."

"I'm just curious," I said, though we both knew better. "Nothing wrong with that."

He sighed, his gaze softening. "Be careful. Whoever did this... they didn't just get lucky."

"I'm always careful," I said, meeting his eyes. "But thanks."

As the remaining stragglers shuffled toward the exits, I saw my chance. Gretchen and Pauline's voices faded into the night as they debated the merits of herbal tea versus hot chocolate for calming Pauline's nerves. Octavian lingered nearby, his sharp eyes scanning the room as though he could read my mind. He wasn't wrong.

"Go ahead without me," I said lightly, gesturing toward the door. "I just want to look around for a minute, make sure no one left their scarf or bag behind."

Octavian didn't look convinced. "Barbara—"

"I'm fine," I assured him, placing a hand on his arm. "Go on."

He hesitated, studying my face like he could peel back the layers of my intentions. Finally, he sighed and nodded. "All right. Take the car. I can easily walk to my house from here. Don't take too long."

"I won't," I said with a reassuring smile.

As he turned and walked away, I felt a pang of guilt but pushed it aside. There wasn't time for hesitation. Once he was out of sight, I moved purposefully through the thinning crowd, weaving toward the evidence bin where the smartwatch now sat, still carefully sealed in that clear plastic bag.

The officers were distracted, their attention

divided between wrapping up their notes and responding to Chief Grimal's barked instructions. One officer had just stepped away from the evidence bin on a table, leaving it momentarily unguarded. This was my window.

I approached casually, my hands gloved and my movements deliberate. Pretending to examine a piece of paper left on the table, I slid my hand into the evidence bin and retrieved the bagged smartwatch. With a quick, practiced motion, I slipped it into the hidden pocket of my jacket and adjusted my scarf for good measure.

No one noticed. Years of training had prepared me for moments like this, and my heart barely raced as I walked away, cool and composed. The faint hum of police radios buzzed in the background, but no one paid me a second glance.

I slipped out of the building through a side exit, the crisp night air hitting my face as I stepped onto the empty sidewalk. The smartwatch felt heavier in my pocket than it should have, its significance pressing against my ribs like a weight. Bryce Thornton's death had been a spectacle, but the truth behind it was quieter, sharper—humming softly in the bagged device tucked under my jacket.

Minutes later, I was seated in my car, the smartwatch resting on the passenger seat in its evidence bag. I glanced around the dark parking lot, ensuring I was alone. Pulling a pair of disposable gloves from my hidden jacket pocket, I slipped them on. Old habits die hard, and I wasn't about to risk exposure to any residue the device might carry.

With practiced care, I removed the smartwatch from the evidence bag, holding it up to the dim glow of the overhead lamp. It looked innocuous—sleek, polished, and overpriced.

The screen flickered to life as I brushed against its side button. A list of options appeared, one of them labeled "Restricted Access." My stomach tightened as I selected it. The screen loaded a sparse, utilitarian interface: a list of encrypted files under a header that read "Access Restricted: Confidential."

Most of the file names were a meaningless jumble of numbers and letters, but one stood out: "TOX-73: Delivery Protocol."

I tapped the file, bracing for the worst. For a split second, I half-expected the watch to lock up or flash a warning message. Instead, a detailed diagram appeared on the screen. It took a moment for my brain to process what I was looking at, and when it did, the realization hit me like a punch to the gut.

The diagram outlined a chemical dispersal

system—compact, efficient, and horrifyingly effective. A small reservoir was integrated into the design, connected to a dispersal mechanism capable of releasing its contents in a controlled radius. Beneath the image, a chilling note read: "Prototype integrated. Testing complete. Deployment authorized."

I stared at the diagram, my pulse quickening. This wasn't just a smartwatch—it was a weapon. Someone had activated it in the middle of Bryce's charity event, turning him into an unwilling test subject.

I leaned back in the seat, the weight of the revelation pressing against my chest. Bryce Thornton was a field test. A live demonstration for whoever was funding this nightmare. If this was only a test, the real deployment would be far worse.

Then I heard it—the unmistakable crunch of boots on gravel. Instinct kicked in, sharp and immediate. My fingers moved quickly, slipping the smartwatch back into its evidence bag and tucking it deep into the side pocket of my jacket.

A moment later, Chief Grimal appeared outside the driver's-side window, his flashlight cutting through the dark. The beam landed briefly on my face, then swept over the car's interior, searching. I rolled the window down slowly, forcing a smile.

"Evening, Chief," I said, my tone light and casual. "What brings you out here?"

"I could ask you the same thing," Grimal replied, his voice gruff. His eyes swept over the interior of the car, lingering briefly on my jacket before locking onto mine. "I thought I saw you sniffing around earlier. Shouldn't you be heading home?"

"Just catching my breath," I replied smoothly. "It's been a strange night."

His scowl deepened. "You weren't touching anything inside, were you? This is a police investigation."

"Investigation?" I echoed, letting sarcasm drip into my tone. "I thought you'd already decided it was a heart attack."

Grimal's jaw tightened, the muscles working visibly beneath his stubble. "Don't push your luck, Barbara. Leave this to the professionals."

"Understood," I said, my voice as sweet as honey. "I wouldn't dream of getting in the way."

Grimal narrowed his eyes, studying me for a beat too long. The flashlight's beam lingered near the jacket pocket where the smartwatch sat. Finally, he sighed, stepping back and gesturing toward the exit.

"Go home, Barbara. And stay out of trouble."

"Always," I replied smoothly, starting the engine

with an even hand. The hum of the car filled the silence as Grimal's shadow loomed in the rearview mirror.

As I pulled out of the parking lot, I could feel the smartwatch's weight in my jacket pocket. Grimal might suspect me, but he didn't have proof. Not yet.

The quiet of the road wrapped around me as I drove, the headlights carving a narrow path through the night. My thoughts raced. Bryce Thornton's death wasn't a random tragedy—it was deliberate, part of something far larger and far more dangerous. Whoever was behind this had underestimated this town.

They hadn't counted on Barbara Gold.

THREE

The morning after Bryce Thornton's death, Cheerville was abuzz with speculation. Bryce's live-streamed collapse had gone viral overnight, spawning hashtags, conspiracy theories, and enough armchair detectives to make the CIA jealous. The internet churned with theories ranging from plausible to absurd. Some swore it was a tragic accident brought on by stress or an undiagnosed condition, while others whispered about sabotage, secret enemies, and even alien interference. The hashtag #WhatKilledBryce trended worldwide, pulling Cheerville into a spotlight it wasn't prepared for.

My phone was constantly buzzing. The senior ladies' group chat, affectionately named "Cheerville's Finest Minds," was in full swing.

Messages from Pauline, Gretchen, and a few others lit up the screen as they dissected last night's drama.

Pauline:

I still don't believe it was a heart attack. Did you SEE his lips?

Gretchen:

Exactly! And the way he grabbed his chest... too theatrical for a heart attack.

Nancy:

You know what they say about these rich types—they're always in trouble. I bet it's something to do with his business deals.

Agnes:

Or maybe it's simpler than that. His last few Instagram posts screamed "stressed out." Didn't he just post about "the future being bright"? That's what people say before things fall apart.

Pauline:

You think it's a coded message?

Agnes:

No, Pauline, I think it's someone trying too hard to look perfect. Big difference.

I shook my head at the mix of wild theories and oddly perceptive observations. Nancy's comment about Bryce's business deals caught my attention, as did Agnes's insight about his posts. While the others debated motives and suspects, I mentally filed away their comments for later. Sometimes, real clues had a habit of slipping through casual chatter.

"Grandma, what are you doing?" Martin asked, breaking my concentration. He was sprawled across my living room floor with a bag of chips, his tablet propped up in front of him and his phone in his left hand. My grandson had taken to hanging out at my house lately, enjoying the relative peace—and, I suspected, the lack of his mother hovering over his shoulder.

"Just chatting with friends," I said.

He sat up and stretched, his sudden movement sent crumbs scattering across the carpet. "Are you chatting about Bryce Thornton?"

I smiled at him in amusement. "How did you know?"

Martin rolled his eyes. "Because everyone is talking about him. Half the school thinks it was sabotage, and the other half thinks he faked his death for attention."

I chuckled. "And what do you think?"

"I think his hashtags are weird," he said, grabbing his phone and scrolling quickly. "Look at this." He held the screen up to me, showing one of Bryce's most recent posts. In it, Bryce was holding up a smartwatch with his signature dazzling smile. The caption read: "The future is bright. #NextLevel #Protocol73."

"That is odd," I said, narrowing my eyes. "What's Protocol 73 supposed to mean?"

Martin shrugged. "No clue. It's not a trending tag. Nobody else uses it except him."

The words sent a chill through me, though I kept my expression neutral. Protocol 73. It couldn't be a coincidence. The file on Bryce's smartwatch—TOX-73: Delivery Protocol—was too similar to ignore. My stomach knotted as I considered the implications. Bryce might have been leaving clues in plain sight— or playing a dangerous game he didn't fully understand.

"Anything else weird?" I asked, leaning closer.

Martin shrugged again, popping another chip into his mouth. "Not really. He was probably trying to start a trend, but it didn't catch on. Influencers do that all the time—throw random hashtags out there and hope something sticks."

I nodded thoughtfully, already piecing together a theory. Bryce might have been using hashtags to promote his brand—or to hide something in plain sight. Either way, it was worth looking into.

The cracks were becoming harder to ignore. If I

wanted to make sense of the hashtag #Protocol73 and its connection to Bryce, I needed to broaden my focus.

"What about Bryce's friends?" I asked, glancing over at Martin. "Didn't he have collaborators? People he worked with?"

Martin shrugged, tossing another chip into his mouth. "I mean, yeah. He's an influencer. They all have friends—or, like, people they pretend are their friends online."

"Anyone specific?" I prompted, keeping my tone light.

Martin grabbed his phone again, scrolling lazily. "I don't follow Bryce, but I know about Fiona Younger. Everyone does."

The name struck a chord. I'd seen her at the auction, the redhead who was talking to that mysterious man. "Fiona Younger," I repeated. "What's her deal?"

Martin looked up from his phone. "She's the second most famous influencer in Cheerville—after Bryce, obviously. They do a ton of collabs together. Giveaways, travel vlogs, stuff like that. She's got a huge following. She's big into lifestyle content—fashion, food, workouts, all that."

"And they worked together often?" I pressed.

"All the time," Martin said, nodding. "People used to ship them as a couple, but they were just friends. She's got her own thing going, though. She doesn't need Bryce to stay relevant."

I tapped my fingers against the armrest of my chair, considering his words. Fiona Younger might not have needed Bryce, but that didn't mean she wasn't connected to whatever trouble he'd been caught up in. If she was the second most famous influencer in Cheerville, she'd likely know more about his personal life than the rest of the town combined. Whether she'd admit it was another matter entirely.

"Anything unusual about her lately?" I asked, trying not to sound too eager.

Martin shrugged again, his focus drifting back to his tablet. "I don't really follow her, but I assume she's still posting a lot of 'day in the life' stuff. Maybe she'll milk the Bryce thing for a while."

I nodded, and pulled out my phone to search for Fiona Younger's accounts.

LATER THAT AFTERNOON, I found myself in Cheerville's town square, scanning the area for

Fiona Younger. After digging through her Insta-gram Lives and TikToks, I'd pieced together her favorite spots in town. It hadn't taken long to find her.

Sure enough, there she was, her camera tripod set up near the fountain, the ring light attached to her phone illuminating her face. She was filming, gesturing animatedly as she narrated to the camera. Her outfit—an oversized scarf, a sleek trench coat, and heeled boots—looked effortless but had likely taken hours to put together. The words "polished perfection" came to mind.

I lingered by a bench, pretending to adjust my tote bag as I watched her wrap up her shoot. She reviewed the footage with a critical eye, her smile fading into a frown as she muttered something to herself. The faint strain in her expression was telling —beneath the polished surface, something was clearly weighing on her.

Fiona was polished, poised, and practiced at saying just enough without giving too much away. But I'd spent years reading people, and there was something about the way her fingers twisted her scarf that told me she wasn't as calm as she wanted me to think.

When she finally packed up her equipment, I

approached, wearing my most disarming smile. "Excuse me, you're Fiona Younger, right?"

She turned, startled, her gaze sweeping over me. "Yes, I am," she said cautiously, her practiced influencer demeanor slipping into place. "Can I help you?"

"I'm so sorry to bother you," I said warmly. "I recognized you from your content. Your posts are always so uplifting."

Her smile softened, the tension in her shoulders easing slightly. "Oh, thank you! That's so kind of you to say. Are you a follower?"

"Yes! And I've seen your collaborations with Bryce Thornton. I wanted to express my condolences. What happened to him was... tragic."

Her face fell, the polished façade cracking. "It's been awful," she said softly. "Bryce was a close friend. I still can't wrap my head around it."

"I can't imagine what you're going through," I said, keeping my voice gentle. "It's such a loss, not just for you but for everyone who knew him. I was hoping you might help me understand what happened. I'd like to do something to honor his memory."

Fiona hesitated, studying me for a moment. "You're not from the press, are you?"

"Not at all," I said with a small laugh. "I'm just a concerned member of the community. Bryce had such an impact on Cheerville—it feels personal.

She sighed, adjusting the strap of her bag sitting down at the fountain. Her movements were slow and deliberate, as though she was weighing her words before speaking. I took it as an invitation and sat beside her, offering an encouraging nod.

"Bryce and I worked together a lot," she began, her voice quiet but steady. "He was brilliant, you know? A visionary. He could make you believe in anything."

"But?" I prompted gently, watching her closely.

She bit her lip, her gaze flicking to the fountain. "But he wasn't afraid to take risks. Big ones. He always thought he was ten steps ahead of everyone else, like nothing could go wrong."

"What kind of risks?" I asked.

Fiona hesitated, twisting her scarf between her fingers. "He got caught up in this tech deal—a huge one. Simon, his business partner, was completely against it. He kept saying it didn't feel right, like something about the whole thing was off, but Bryce wouldn't listen. He thought it was his chance to change everything."

My interest sharpened. "What kind of deal was it?"

Fiona shook her head. "I don't know the details, but it was tied to their company, Thornton & Kane. Bryce was trying to launch something revolutionary, and Simon didn't want to be involved. They fought about it constantly."

"What happened next?"

She sighed, her shoulders slumping. "Simon finally gave up and let him do it. But then Bryce died."

"Was Simon at the auction?"

"Yes. I was with him and he had to watch his friend die like the rest of us. Last I heard, Simon went on vacation."

"Vacation?" I asked, raising an eyebrow.

Fiona's lips tightened. "That's what he called it. But honestly? It feels more like he wanted to lie low until everything settled down. He wasn't happy about what Bryce got mixed up in, and I think he just wanted to get as far away from it all as he could."

Her words hung in the air, heavy with implication. She glanced at me, hesitating, then continued.

"Maybe I shouldn't even be talking about this," she murmured, her voice dropping. "I don't want to start rumors, especially if there's nothing to it. But..."

She gave a small, wry smile, her shoulders relaxing slightly. "No offense, you seem harmless enough. Like the kind of person I could tell anything to."

I smiled faintly, my expression neutral. "I appreciate that, Fiona. Bryce seemed like someone with big ideas. It sounds like he had a lot of passion for what he was doing."

She nodded, though her brows furrowed slightly. "He did. But Simon couldn't shake the feeling that something was going to go wrong. He wasn't the type to panic, you know? But when it came to this deal, he couldn't stop saying how bad it felt."

"And Bryce?"

Fiona sighed again. "He just kept going. He said Simon was being paranoid, that every big idea comes with risks. He wouldn't even consider stopping."

"Do you suspect Bryce's death was related to this business deal?"

She shook her head. "I really don't know. Maybe I don't want to know, if it's really as dangerous as Simon thinks."

"Thank you, Fiona," I said sincerely. "I appreciate you taking the time to talk with me."

Her words lingered as I rose, the afternoon sunlight casting long shadows across the square.

"I just miss him," she said softly, her hands tightening on her bag. "I hope whatever this was, it's over now."

"I hope so too," I replied, though I didn't believe it for a second.

LATER THAT EVENING, I found myself walking up the neatly paved path to Octavian's house. The cool night air carried the faint scent of blooming flowers from his tidy garden, the rows of neatly trimmed hedges framing the pathway like a green welcome mat. His porch light cast a soft, inviting glow over the well-maintained lawn, and the faint sound of smooth jazz drifted through the open window, weaving its way into the stillness of the night. A smile tugged at my lips as I approached the door. Octavian had a knack for making even the simplest moments feel effortlessly inviting, as though every detail were part of a carefully planned scene.

I knocked lightly, the sound blending with the muted rhythm of the music inside. Moments later, the door swung open, revealing Octavian with an apron tied over his crisp button-up shirt and that signature warm smile of his. "You're just in time," he said, stepping aside to let me in. "I was about to drain the pasta."

"It smells divine already," I replied, the rich, comforting aroma of fresh bread mingling with the savory notes of whatever sauce he had simmering on the stove. As I shrugged off my jacket and hung it neatly on the nearby rack, the familiar air of Octavian's home enveloped me. His space always radiated a blend of comfort and sophistication, the kind of place where every corner seemed to invite you to linger just a little longer.

"Come on, let me show you what I've been working on," he said, leading me toward the kitchen. The soft light from the pendant lamp above the table illuminated a perfect setting for two. Plates, glasses, and silverware were arranged with precision, and at the center of the table sat a bottle of red wine, its cork removed and the liquid breathing in anticipation of the meal. The scene was quintessentially Octavian— thoughtful and effortlessly elegant.

"Let me pour you a glass," he offered, grabbing the wine bottle and filling two glasses with a practiced ease that hinted at years of hosting. "You can chop the parsley if you'd like to earn your keep."

I smirked, picking up the knife from the chopping board. "You've got a deal. But don't expect perfection—it's been a while since I held a knife for something as innocent as herbs."

He grinned as he rolled up his sleeves, checking the sauce bubbling gently on the stove. "I'll take my chances. But I have to say, you look pleased with yourself tonight. What mischief have you been up to?"

Setting the knife down after a few clumsy chops, I glanced at him with a wry smile. "Mischief? Hardly. I've joined the modern age."

"Oh?" he said, raising an eyebrow as he stirred the sauce with deliberate, fluid motions. The curiosity in his tone was impossible to miss.

I took my glass and leaned against the counter, a grin spreading across my face. "I made an Instagram account. With Martin's help, of course."

Octavian paused, his expression morphing into amused disbelief. He turned to face me fully, his wooden spoon poised mid-air. "You? On social media? Now that's something I never thought I'd see. What's your handle? SpyGram69?"

I rolled my eyes, though a chuckle escaped despite my best efforts to appear unamused. "Very funny. It's not for me—it's for Dandelion. She's the star of the show."

That caught him off guard, and his laughter filled

the kitchen. "Your cat? You made an account for your cat?"

"Of course," I replied, enjoying the incredulity on his face. "Cats are internet gold. Martin said it was the easiest way to get followers without actually trying. So far, she's already got twenty likes on her first post."

Octavian shook his head, still chuckling as he carried a tray of garlic bread to the table. "What kind of content are we talking here? Cat memes? Fashion shoots? Product endorsements?"

"A bit of everything," I said breezily, lifting the chopped parsley and sprinkling it into a small bowl. "Her first post is a regal shot of her on the windowsill. Caption: 'Queen of the Castle.'"

"Naturally," he replied with a grin, taking a sip of wine as he leaned against the counter. "Dandelion's always had an air of royalty. I imagine she'll be demanding her own line of merch soon."

"Don't tempt me," I said, smirking at the idea of Dandelion-branded mugs and T-shirts. "But seriously, it's just for fun. And, well... research."

Octavian's smile faltered slightly, his gaze softening as he studied me. "Research, hmm? Barbara, you know I adore you, but you have a knack for turning harmless fun into... well, not-so-harmless adventures."

"It's harmless," I assured him, though the flicker of skepticism in his eyes suggested he wasn't entirely convinced. I held his gaze for a moment, maintaining a steady expression, but the hint of amusement in the corner of his mouth didn't escape me.

He leaned back in his chair, swirling his wine thoughtfully before lifting the glass to his lips. "Promise me one thing," he said, his tone lighter but still carrying an edge of seriousness. "Don't get into too much trouble. Cheerville has enough excitement without you stirring the pot."

I clinked my glass gently against his, a faint smile tugging at the corners of my mouth. "You know me, Octavian. I'm the picture of caution."

"That's what I'm afraid of," he replied with a chuckle, shaking his head as he turned back to the stove to plate the pasta. The scent of the rich sauce filled the air, mingling with the comforting warmth of the garlic bread.

As he carried the steaming plates to the table, the easy rhythm of our banter continued, weaving seamlessly into the evening.

FOUR

For someone who fancied herself social-media-averse, I was spending an alarming amount of time buried in Bryce Thornton's Instagram profile. From my cozy spot on the living room couch, I scrolled past his carefully curated posts, taking mental notes. Bryce's feed was a shrine to his polished persona: sunlit selfies, luxurious backdrops, and captions dripping with charm. His entire online presence screamed aspiration and perfection, every detail meticulously crafted to present a life most people could only dream of. Dandelion purred contentedly beside me, occasionally swatting at my notebook as though trying to add her own insights to the investigation. Her tail flicked across the page, smudging one of my neatly circled hashtags

"Not helpful," I muttered, nudging her gently away. She responded by flopping dramatically onto her side, as if to say, *Fine, I'll let you do it your way*.

Martin was on the other end of the couch, his legs stretched out and a bag of his favorite chips resting precariously on the arm of the couch. He scrolled through TikTok with the energy and efficiency only a teenager could muster, pausing occasionally to snort at a particularly ridiculous video. The faint crunch of chips and the occasional hum of a trending TikTok song filled the otherwise quiet room.

"Bryce's TikTok is weird," Martin announced suddenly, his tone somewhere between intrigue and mild irritation. "It's, like, half dance trends and half product demos."

I glanced over at him, raising an eyebrow. "Weird how? What kind of demos?"

"Like, tech stuff. But it's all super staged," he said, wrinkling his nose. "He's trying to make it look casual, but it's so fake. Nobody actually talks about 'life-changing innovation' while doing a bad Renegade."

I chuckled softly, flipping to a fresh page in my notebook. "Every audience is different. Maybe he was appealing to multiple markets. Isn't that what influencers do?"

Martin snorted, rolling his eyes. "Yeah, markets with no taste. It's cringe, Grandma."

Dandelion stretched lazily beside me, letting out a faint meow as if agreeing with him. I scratched behind her ears absentmindedly, my attention drawn to another post of Bryce's. This one featured him holding the smartwatch, his smile dazzling as ever. The caption read: "The future is here. #Protocol73." I jotted the hashtag down in my notes, circling it for emphasis.

"Anything interesting?" Martin asked, glancing up briefly from his phone.

"This hashtag you mentioned #Protocol73 keeps showing up on his tech-related posts," I said casually. "Does it show up a lot on his TikTok?"

Martin tilted his head, his fingers flying across his phone as he searched. "Let me see... yeah, but not a lot. It's not trending or anything."

"Hmm," I murmured, tapping my pen against the notebook. "So he was trying to make it a thing, but it didn't take off?"

"Looks like it," Martin said, popping another chip into his mouth. "He probably thought it sounded cool, but it's kind of lame."

Protocol 73. The name alone carried weight, echoing the encrypted files I'd found on the smart-watch. The pieces were starting to fit together, but the picture they formed was far from clear. Bryce's carefully curated image didn't leave much room for ambiguity, yet here he was using a hashtag that seemed deliberately cryptic. It didn't fit his usual style.

"Anything else unusual about his posts?" I asked, leaning closer.

Martin shrugged, scrolling absently through his phone. "Not really. Just feels like he was trying way too hard, you know? Like he wanted to make everything look perfect, but it comes off... desperate."

He ate another chip before returning to his endless scroll of videos. Dandelion jumped onto his chest, curling up as though claiming him for a nap.

"You know, Grandma," Martin said, stroking Dandelion's fur. "If you want your account to take off, you need a strategy. Hashtags aren't just for decoration."

I raised an eyebrow. "Oh? And what do you suggest, Mr. Social Media Expert?"

He leaned forward, the glint of excitement in his eyes unmistakable. "First off, you need to post more. One picture of Dandelion isn't going to cut it. People want content—variety. You've got to give them action shots, funny captions, maybe even a reel or two. Reels are huge right now."

Dandelion swished her tail as if to emphasize his point. I scratched her ears, pretending to consider his advice. "Reels, hmm? I'll add that to my to-do list."

Martin sighed dramatically, like a teacher trying to explain basic arithmetic to a particularly dense student. "I'm serious, Grandma. And don't forget hashtags. You need stuff like #CatsOfInstagram and #FluffyQueen. That's how people find your account. Trust me, it's all about discoverability."

"Fluffy Queen?" I repeated, stifling a laugh. "I'll take it under advisement."

He shrugged, clearly pleased with himself. "Just trying to help you go viral."

I smiled indulgently, my focus drifting back to Bryce's Instagram feed. His curated photos made me roll my eyes inwardly, but I knew better than to dismiss Martin's enthusiasm outright. He was in his element, and that kind of confidence was worth indulging—for now.

"Honestly, Grandma," he said, his grin widening as he leaned closer, "if you want this account to blow up, you should just let me handle it. I know what works."

I raised an eyebrow, pretending to consider his offer. "Oh, really? And you'd do all the work?"

"Obviously," he replied. "You can't expect Dandelion to go viral with you running things. No offense, but your last post was... kind of boring."

Dandelion, as if sensing she was the topic of conversation, stretched luxuriously on the empty space on the couch between us, her tail flicking lazily as she yawned. Her emerald-green eyes narrowed briefly before closing.

"Fine," I said. "If you're so confident, the account is yours—for now. Just don't do anything embarrassing. Dandelion has a reputation to uphold."

Martin's face lit up as if I'd just handed him the keys to a sports car. His phone was already in his hand, his thumbs flying over the screen. "This is going to be epic," he said, his tone brimming with anticipation. "I've got so many ideas. First, we'll need a signature look for Dandelion. Maybe a hat. Or a tiny crown. People love cats in costumes."

"A crown?" I echoed, half-laughing. "Dandelion's not exactly the cooperative type."

"We'll work on it," he said dismissively, his attention fully absorbed by whatever he was planning. "I'll start with a series—something catchy, like 'Dandelion's Daily Adventures.' Trust me, Grandma, this account is going places."

I shook my head, amused by his enthusiasm. "Just remember, it's not about quantity. Quality matters too."

"Yeah, yeah," he said, waving me off. "Let the pro handle it."

Dandelion, as if deciding to humor him, leapt down from the couch and strutted across the room, her tail held high. Martin immediately turned his phone toward her, capturing the moment like a wildlife photographer spotting a rare species. "See? She's a natural. This is going to be gold."

I chuckled as I watched him work. The house filled with the quiet sounds of camera shutters and Dandelion's occasional meows, her regal indifference providing the perfect foil to Martin's uncontainable energy. For the first time in days, the tension in my chest eased slightly. If nothing else, this little project would keep Martin occupied—and Dandelion wouldn't mind the extra attention.

"This is going to be epic. I've got so many ideas!"

He jumped to his feet, his camera poised and ready, while Dandelion watched him with her usual air of feline indifference. Settling into a crouch, Martin brought the lens to eye level with her. "Okay,

Dandelion, work with me here. Look regal. You're a queen."

I chuckled, glancing up from my cup of tea. Dandelion blinked slowly, her green eyes half-lidded, and gave a long stretch, utterly unimpressed with Martin's direction.

"You might need to refine your skills, Martin. She's not exactly radiating enthusiasm."

"You just have to understand her vibe," Martin replied confidently. "She's a diva. Divas take their time. Watch this."

He adjusted his angle, capturing her from above as the sunlight streaming through the window lit her fur like a golden halo. Dandelion yawned, the motion surprisingly graceful, and Martin grinned triumphantly. "See? Look at this shot."

He turned the screen toward me, and I had to admit, the close-up was striking. The sunlight caught the emerald flecks in her eyes perfectly, her fur glowing like she'd stepped out of an artfully lit studio.

"Not bad," I said.

Martin's fingers flew over the keyboard as he narrated dramatically. "'Bow before your queen. #CatsOfInstagram #FluffyQueen #Purrfection.'"

I laughed, shaking my head. "Fluffy Queen

strikes again. You're going to have to keep this momentum going, you know. Dandelion has a brand to maintain now."

"Please," Martin said with a smirk. "This is just the beginning. Wait until I get her to model with props."

Switching to video mode, Martin dangled a feather toy in front of Dandelion, his voice rising slightly in excitement. "Okay, action shot time. Let's see what you've got, Dandelion."

To my surprise, Dandelion batted at the toy with an almost theatrical swat, her movements slow but deliberate, as though she knew exactly how to keep her audience entertained. Martin gasped like he'd just discovered the eighth wonder of the world. "This is gold. Pure gold."

He followed her movements with the camera, narrating like a wildlife documentarian. "Notice how the regal predator stalks her prey. The precision. The elegance. She is... unstoppable."

I leaned back in my chair, thoroughly entertained. "National Geographic would be proud."

Martin shot me a mock-serious look. "You joke, but just wait. By the end of the week, she'll have a hundred followers. Minimum. Maybe even go viral."

Dandelion leapt to swat the toy again, this time

landing a dramatic spin that sent her tail flicking. Martin caught it perfectly on video, his laugh echoing through the room. "Okay, that's it. This one's going on TikTok."

As the sun dipped below the horizon, casting long shadows across the kitchen, Martin continued his creative streak, snapping photos of Dandelion lounging on the table like a queen surveying her domain. I let his enthusiasm fill the space, enjoying the rare glimpse of him so animated and engaged.

When Martin finally paused for a break, his phone buzzing with likes and comments from his first post, I returned to my phone. Bryce Thornton's Instagram feed was still open, a stark contrast to Dandelion's whimsical content. The polished perfection of his posts felt hollow now, each caption a potential breadcrumb leading to the truth.

I picked up my notebook, already filled with scribbled notes and half-formed ideas. The hashtags Bryce had used—#Protocol73, #GameChanger, #NewWorldOrder—took on an ominous weight, the words swirling in my mind as I jotted down connections that refused to stay clear.

Dandelion, apparently satisfied with her photoshoot, curled up next to my notebook, her tail flicking lazily against the pages. Her warmth was a small comfort against the unease settling in my chest.

"You might be a star now, but I've still got work to do," I murmured, scratching her behind the ears. She purred softly, her eyes narrowing as if to agree.

Bryce was gone, but his posts remained. And somewhere in those curated images and cryptic hashtags lay the key to unraveling the same shadowy world that had taken his life.

FIVE

Early the next morning, when I was alone again, the house was quiet except for the faint hum of the laptop I'd retrieved from its hiding spot in the attic. Its sleek, matte black surface showed no signs of age, but I could feel the years of dust it had gathered in its dormant state. Most people in Cheerville had laptops or tablets, but this wasn't just any computer —it was a relic from my old life, custom-built for situations exactly like this. Every component had been chosen for speed, security, and stealth. I hadn't touched it in years, but as the screen flickered to life, I felt the same surge of focus I used to feel in the field, as though the years between then and now had vanished in an instant.

Dandelion leapt onto the desk, her tail flicking as she was about to bend down and sniff at the sleek smartwatch resting beside the keyboard. "Not for you," I murmured, nudging her gently away.

She sat down, watching me with mild disapproval. Her eyes tracked every movement of my hands, as if ready to offer pointers should I falter. For all her feline arrogance, I felt a strange comfort in her presence. She was my only witness to this secret revival of my old skills, a quiet reminder of the double life I continued to lead.

I turned the watch over in my hands, noting its unremarkable exterior. No engravings, no hidden compartments—just smooth, polished metal and a darkened screen. Its simplicity was deceptive, masking the secrets it held. Plugging it into the laptop with a universal connector cable, I tapped a few keys and brought up its interface. The files began to load, their progress bar crawling across the screen. The steady rhythm of the loading bar was almost hypnotic, like the metronome to a high-stakes symphony.

The first few folders were disappointingly mundane—fitness logs, GPS data, and syncing records. Nothing unusual. I scanned through them briefly, noting the ordinary metrics of an ordinary life. But as I scrolled further, I spotted a folder labeled "Secure" in bold. Clicking it brought up a password prompt, along with a cryptic hint: "Cloud access required."

I frowned, leaning back in my chair. Cloud access. Of course. The smartwatch wasn't just a standalone device—it was linked to a remote account. Whatever secrets Bryce Thornton had locked away weren't stored locally; they were in the cloud. If someone else had access to the same account, they could already be covering their tracks.

Dandelion let out a soft meow, almost as if sensing my frustration. I reached over to scratch behind her ears, more to steady my nerves than anything else. Her soft purring reminded me that patience was a virtue—a virtue that, even now, I was still trying to master. With a deep breath, I turned my focus back to the screen. If Bryce's secrets were in the cloud, I would need to think a few steps ahead to retrieve them before they vanished forever.

"Okay, girl," I murmured, scratching behind her ears in slow, deliberate strokes. Dandelion leaned into my hand, her purring growing louder, a rhythmic hum of contentment that somehow seemed to fill the quiet space around us. "We're just getting started." Her tail flicked lazily as if to say she wasn't entirely convinced by my words, but she settled down beside me, curling into a warm, compact bundle of fur.

Turning my attention back to the screen, I entered a few more keystrokes, scanning the watch's memory for any stored credentials. The faint hum of the laptop was the only sound in the room, a low and steady backdrop to my work. Sure enough, a cached login attempt popped up—a username containing Bryce's initials. A small sense of triumph stirred in me at the discovery, but it was short-lived. The password, of course, was encrypted. That part wasn't surprising, but it didn't make it any less frustrating.

Cracking the encryption would take time, so I set the laptop to work. The decryption tool began its task, its status bar creeping forward with an almost taunting slowness. The faint whirring sound of the software at work was oddly soothing, a mechanical reminder that progress, however slow, was being made.

While the program did its job, I decided to revisit the smartwatch's logs. It wasn't a particularly large memory cache, but I scrolled through the data carefully, piece by piece, looking for anything I might

have missed. A few details caught my attention—
Bluetooth connections to nearby devices, location
pings from the night of the auction, and an unex-
plained surge in activity just before Bryce collapsed.
The timestamps and metadata painted a picture that
wasn't quite clear yet, but the outlines of something
important were there. I jotted everything down in
my notebook, writing with deliberate precision. Each
connection, every timestamp, and every anomaly was
underlined and circled for later investigation.

The soft ding of the decryption tool pulled me
out of my thoughts, its cheerful tone startling in the
otherwise quiet room. My eyes snapped back to the
laptop, where the password now appeared on the
screen, a seemingly random mix of numbers and
letters. A slow smile spread across my face as I carefully copied it down into my notebook. The jumble
of characters felt like the first tangible piece of the
puzzle falling into place.

Returning to the cloud access prompt, I pasted
the password in. After I hit "Enter," the tension in
my chest tightened as I waited for the next step, a
mix of anticipation and determination washing
over me.

The page loaded slowly, the spinning wheel
mocking my patience as I stared at the screen. The

seconds dragged into what felt like minutes. I tapped my fingers lightly on the desk, the rhythm syncing with the soft hum of the laptop's fan.

When the page finally opened, a folder labeled "Protocol 73" sat at the top of the directory. My stomach tightened at the sight of it, an involuntary reaction to the name itself. Without hesitation, I moved the cursor to the folder and clicked it open.

Inside was a collection of files, their titles chillingly specific: "TOX-73 Deployment Specs," "Field Test Logs," and "Activation Protocol." Each name carried weight, heavy with implication, but my attention was immediately drawn to a small symbol in the corner of the file directory. A triangle intersected by a diagonal line. My breath caught in my throat, and for a moment, the room seemed to chill. That symbol.

The sight of it sent a shiver down my spine. Back in my CIA days, it had been linked to a tech syndicate dabbling in espionage and black-market trading. They were amateurs back then, operating in shadows too dim for major players to notice. More nuisance than threat, they hadn't warranted more than cursory attention. But now, seeing their mark here, connected to something as serious as Protocol 73, suggested they'd graduated beyond those small-time beginnings. They'd grown, evolved, and their ambitions had clearly taken a darker turn.

My hand hovered over the trackpad for a moment before I clicked on the file labeled "Field Test Logs." The file opened slowly, the spinning wheel making another appearance, as though to prolong the dread clawing its way into my chest. When the contents finally appeared, my worst fears were confirmed. A detailed report filled the screen, outlining a series of experiments conducted with the smartwatch's dispersal mechanism. Each entry was painstakingly documented: the date, location, dispersal radius, and chemical used. The clinical precision of the logs was chilling, each line devoid of emotion yet brimming with sinister intent.

At the bottom of the most recent entry, a note stood out in stark relief: "Field test successful. Deployment ready." The words struck me like a physical blow, leaving me momentarily breathless.

Bryce Thornton had indeed been a test subject. Someone had used him to prove the smartwatch's capabilities, treating his life as a mere variable in their equations. And now, the system was operational. The technology was ready. The implications were terrifying. If they could do this to Bryce, they could do it to anyone.

Dandelion stretched lazily across the table, her paw nudging the notebook I'd been scribbling in, as though to dismiss my concerns entirely. Her calm indifference to the unfolding nightmare made me smile faintly, even as my thoughts churned. "You're right," I said softly, scratching her chin with one hand while flipping a page in my notebook with the other. "There's more to this. We're just scratching the surface." Her purr rumbled gently, a small reminder that not everything in the world was tainted with danger. But the look I gave the screen was resolute. I wasn't about to stop now.

As the day stretched on, I learned more from the encrypted files. Each revelation unraveled a deeper layer of the truth, and with it, the weight of what Protocol 73 represented pressed down on me. This wasn't just a weapon—it was a scalpel for chaos, capable of bringing entire systems to their knees with terrifying precision.

A program designed to infiltrate and disable systems remotely, it was the kind of tool that could bring entire infrastructures to their knees. Financial networks could be breached in seconds, their data corrupted or accounts drained. Power grids could be disabled, plunging cities into darkness and chaos. Even transportation hubs could be disrupted, grounding planes and halting trains in an instant. The sheer breadth of its potential destruction was staggering. No aspect of modern life was beyond its reach.

The logs were disturbingly meticulous. Each file detailed how these systems could be infiltrated and dismantled with precision, listing vulnerabilities like a grim instruction manual for chaos. Every step was laid out in cold, emotionless text, describing a series of actions that could cripple entire nations in a matter of minutes. It wasn't just the potential for destruction that unnerved me—it was the calculated efficiency of it all. This wasn't a crude or hastily constructed plan; it was the work of experts, and its creators knew exactly what they were doing.

I leaned back in my chair, staring at the screen as the enormity of it all sunk in. Did Bryce Thornton really not know what he was getting into? Did he truly believe this technology would help people instead of hurt them? Or was he simply too blinded by ambition, by the promise of success and innovation, to see the truth? Whatever he believed, it didn't matter anymore. His role in this was finished. He had been a pawn in their game, an unwitting accomplice who helped secure their funding.

Maybe they were making an example of him to

keep their other investors in line. Like Simon Kane. The thoughts and theories lingered as I turned back to the laptop. The files had painted a picture of something far more sinister than I could have imagined, and I needed to understand the scope of what I was dealing with.

I opened up a private browser, my fingers moving across the keyboard with practiced precision, and pulled up LuxTech's official website. The homepage loaded quickly, a polished facade that practically gleamed with professionalism and trustworthiness. Bold text splashed across the screen: "Technology That Connects Us." It was the kind of slogan that would have reassured anyone, promising innovation with a friendly, forward-thinking ethos.

Beneath the tagline, promotional videos played in a seamless loop. They showcased LuxTech's flagship products: smartwatches, fitness trackers, and health monitors. Happy families, smiling professionals, and carefree athletes filled the screen, each one perfectly framed to emphasize convenience and wellness. Everything about the site screamed modernity, innovation, and reliability. If I hadn't already known what the smartwatch was truly capable of, I might have been impressed. It was easy to see how someone like Bryce could have been drawn in, lured by the promise of being part of something ground-breaking. But knowing what I now knew, the entire presentation felt like a mask, hiding the dangers lurking beneath the surface.

I scrolled down the page, letting the videos and text blur past as I searched for something more concrete. Then, a bright, bold announcement caught my eye, standing out against the sleek background: "Join Us at the Cheerville TechXpo!" The words practically leaped off the screen. My stomach tightened as I read the details. If this was where LuxTech was showcasing their technology, it could also be where their plans were advancing. I didn't need to read the fine print to know that Cheerville TechXpo was about to become my next target.

The expo was scheduled for the end of the week, with LuxTech listed as a primary sponsor. The website boasted that this would be their most significant showcase yet, promising to unveil a ground-breaking line of wearable technology designed to "revolutionize connectivity."

Even after what had happened to Bryce, they still had the gall to show up in Cheerville, flaunting their supposed innovations without a hint of remorse. It was a bold move, almost taunting, as if they believed themselves untouchable.

Dandelion stretched lazily across the table, her small paw nudging my notebook in an unspoken demand for attention. I reached out and scratched under her chin, earning a soft purr for my trouble. "I know," I murmured, my gaze fixed on the screen. "We need to figure out what they're planning." Her contented rumble filled the air, a brief respite from the heaviness of the task ahead, but it didn't lessen the weight pressing on my chest.

I navigated to the expo's official website, scanning the list of sponsors and exhibitors. The page was slick and polished, designed to attract both investors and attendees. LuxTech's logo was prominently displayed at the top, its sleek design and tagline standing out like a crown jewel. Beneath it was a glowing description of their contributions to the tech industry, full of phrases like "trailblazing innovations" and "reshaping the future.

Further down the page, I found a map of the event layout. The exhibition hall was divided into rows of booths, each with its own assigned number and label. Booth 27, listed as "LuxTech Wearable Innovations," was right in the center of the main exhibition hall. A prime location, no doubt chosen to ensure maximum visibility and foot traffic.

Clicking back to LuxTech's official site, I

searched for more information about their leadership. The page loaded quickly, presenting me with a curated list of executives, each with a professional photo and a polished biography. At the top was the CEO, a man with sharp features and a practiced smile, the kind of image designed to instill confidence and trust in shareholders. Below him was a collection of other executives, marketing directors, and a PR team whose primary job was to ensure that LuxTech's image remained pristine. But as I scrolled through the names and faces, nothing leaped out at me—no immediate connections to Bryce Thornton or Simon Kane. It was as if the people behind this operation had gone out of their way to maintain a façade of legitimacy.

Then, as my eyes scanned the menu bar, I spotted a subpage titled "Our Partners." Curiosity piqued, I clicked the link, and a grid of logos and descriptions appeared on the screen. Most of the names were unfamiliar, representing a mix of tech firms and startups that had collaborated with LuxTech on various projects. But nestled among them was a name I recognized immediately: Thornton & Kane.

My pulse quickened as I clicked on the link. The page that loaded detailed a partnership between

LuxTech and Bryce's company to develop a "revolutionary wearable platform." Bryce Thornton and Simon Kane had worked closely with LuxTech on the smartwatch project. They were key players in bringing this technology to life.

Simon Kane. Fiona had mentioned that he'd been skeptical about the deal, claiming it didn't sit right with him. He had argued against it, insisting something about the partnership felt wrong. And yet, he hadn't been able to stop it. Now, just days after Bryce's death, Simon had conveniently gone on vacation—or more likely, he had decided to lie low until the dust settled. Whatever was happening, it was clear Simon Kane knew more than he was letting on. He was running scared, and I didn't blame him.

Dandelion let out a soft, almost questioning meow, her green eyes fixed on me as if she could sense the wheels turning in my mind. I reached out again, my fingers brushing through her fur. "I know," I said softly. "The expo's the next step. Cheerville is still their testing ground. If they're unveiling more devices, and selling them to everyone now, there's no telling how far this could go."

She meowed again, almost as if voicing her agreement—or perhaps just asking for more attention.

"Well, Dandelion," I said with a faint smile,

scratching the soft spot between her ears. "Looks like we've got our work cut out for us." Her purring intensified, a quiet reassurance that I wasn't in this alone. Even if my only ally at the moment had four legs and a tendency to interrupt, it was enough to keep me moving forward.

SIX

The late morning sun cast a warm, golden glow over Cheerville as I made my way to Lucky Dragon, the town's beloved Chinese takeout spot. The light filtered through the trees lining the main street, dappling the sidewalk with shifting patterns that danced in time with the breeze. Even from a distance, the Lucky Dragon's cheerful red-and-gold sign stood out against the muted tones of the other shops, a beacon for hungry locals seeking solace in its familiar fare.

The small, unassuming restaurant was more than just a place to grab a quick meal—it was a Cheerville institution, a cornerstone of the town's charm and routine. For Chief Grimal, it was practically a second home. If he wasn't picking up takeout, he was dining in, savoring his favorites like sweet-and-sour chicken or pork fried rice.

As I approached the door, the faint clang of pots and pans from the kitchen mingled with the hum of the lunchtime crowd inside, creating a lively backdrop of activity. Stepping inside, the familiar chime of the bell above the door greeted me, accompanied by the unmistakable aroma of freshly cooked dishes. The scent alone was enough to make my stomach rumble, and I silently reminded myself to avoid ordering half the menu. Lucky Dragon's warm, wood-paneled walls and the soft glow of red paper lanterns overhead gave it a cozy, timeless charm.

I scanned the room, letting my eyes adjust to the softer light inside. It didn't take long to spot him: Chief Grimal, seated at his usual corner table, a half-empty plate of sweet-and-sour chicken in front of him alongside a mound of fried rice and a pot of tea. His figure was unmistakable, the familiar outline of his shoulders slightly hunched as he focused on a stack of papers he'd brought along. It was a typical scene, one I'd witnessed countless times. Grimal's love for Lucky Dragon's food was no secret; I'd once heard someone joke that the restaurant should have a plaque with his name on it.

He didn't see me, his attention entirely

consumed by the meal and whatever work he was reviewing. The faint furrow in his brow suggested his mind was elsewhere. I hesitated for a moment, debating whether to approach him right away or take my time. Ultimately, I decided to play it cool. There was no need to rush.

Making my way to the counter, I was greeted by a familiar, friendly face. May Lee, the restaurant's longtime owner, stood behind the counter, her bright green apron dusted with flour from the dumplings she had clearly been prepping earlier.

"Barbara! Dining in today?" she asked, her tone as cheerful as ever.

"Just takeout today, May," I replied, returning her smile. "Shrimp lo mein. Oh, and add an order of egg rolls to that, please."

"Coming right up," she said, jotting the order down on her notepad.

When she disappeared to the kitchen to quickly give the cooks my order, I took the opportunity to glance back at Grimal. He was now reaching for his tea, his eyes still glued to the papers in front of him. His obliviousness brought a small smile to my face. For all his bluster and posturing as Cheerville's chief of police, he was never more vulnerable—or more predictable—than when he was here, tucked away in his corner at Lucky Dragon.

After I paid and May handed me my receipt, I asked, "Mind if I wait over there until my order's ready?" I gestured toward a table near Grimal's, keeping my tone light and casual, as if the spot I'd chosen was completely arbitrary.

"Of course," she said brightly, wiping her hands on her apron. "It shouldn't be too long. Just a few minutes."

"Perfect," I replied, tucking the receipt into my purse. I took a moment to perform glancing around the restaurant as though considering my options, then made my way toward Grimal's table. My pace was deliberately unhurried, my steps measured. I let my expression settle into one of pleasant surprise.

"Chief Grimal," I greeted warmly, coming to a stop just beside his table. "Fancy running into you here."

He looked up from his plate, his brows knitting together for a brief moment at the interruption. "Barbara," he said, setting down his chopsticks and leaning back slightly. His eyes narrowed, though not unkindly. "You're everywhere, aren't you?"

"Oh, I could say the same about you," I replied

with a light laugh, gesturing toward his table and the food spread before him. "But then again, who could resist Lucky Dragon's sweet-and-sour chicken?"

"They do it better than anyone," he admitted, though his tone remained guarded. His chopsticks hovered over his plate, poised for the next bite but momentarily stalled. "What brings you here?"

"Lunch," I said simply, as though the answer were obvious. "Shrimp lo mein and egg rolls. You know, the classics. But I didn't expect to find Cheerville's finest holding court over fried rice."

A small snort escaped him. He gestured toward the stack of papers beside him, his chopsticks finally moving to pluck another piece of chicken from the plate. "Even I need a break sometimes."

"Well, don't let me interrupt," I said lightly, though I made no move to leave. Instead, I shifted my weight slightly, lingering just long enough to signal that I wasn't entirely ready to part ways. "But if you're open to company, I wouldn't mind sitting for a bit while I wait for my order."

He hesitated, his gaze flicking from me to the empty chair across the table, then back again. For a moment, it seemed like he might decline, but finally, with a small shrug, he relented. "Suit yourself."

Sliding into the seat, I settled in comfortably.

"It's been ages since I've eaten here," I said, letting a note of nostalgia creep into my voice. "I forgot how good it smells. The place hasn't changed a bit."

"Smells good, tastes better," he replied, his tone softening slightly as he scooped up another bite of rice and returned his focus to his meal. It wasn't quite an invitation to continue the conversation, but it wasn't a dismissal either.

I let the hum of the restaurant fill the brief silence between us, the clatter of dishes and the murmur of nearby conversations creating a comfortable backdrop. My presence was unobtrusive, patient, as if I was perfectly content to sit quietly and wait for my food. Then, with just the right touch of curiosity, I leaned forward slightly, resting my forearms lightly on the table.

"I hope work isn't keeping you too busy," I said, my voice casual but laced with genuine interest. "You must be swamped with everything going on around town these days."

He didn't look up from his plate, his expression remaining neutral. "Trouble's part of the job," he replied flatly, his tone suggesting it was a sentiment he repeated often, one he had long since resigned himself to.

"Let me guess," I said, lowering my voice

conspiratorially as I leaned more, as though we were two colleagues trading secrets. "Bryce Thornton?"

Grimal's jaw tightened ever so slightly, a flicker of tension that didn't go unnoticed. It wasn't much, but it was enough to confirm I'd hit a nerve. Still, he didn't shut me down immediately, which I took as a small victory. "Why do you ask?" he replied, his tone cautious but not yet defensive.

"Oh, no reason," I said lightly, adding a nonchalant shrug for good measure. "It's just that everyone seems to be talking about it. You know how it is in Cheerville—news travels fast, and people love to gossip." I gave him an easy smile, as if to say I was just another curious townsperson, no deeper motives here.

Grimal didn't return the smile, but his expression remained measured, his eyes watching me closely. "People always speculate," he said after a moment, his voice even and deliberate. "Doesn't mean they're right."

"Of course not," I agreed quickly, keeping my tone agreeable and my posture relaxed. I tilted my head as though mulling something over, adding just a touch of curiosity to my expression. "But you have to admit, it's a bit unusual. A young, healthy man like

Bryce, collapsing so suddenly? It's no wonder folks are buzzing about it."

Grimal set his chopsticks down with deliberate care. His gaze sharpened, cutting through the casual atmosphere I'd tried to maintain. From the kitchen, the clang of a wok echoed loudly, followed by the hiss of something hitting hot oil, momentarily filling the space between us. I said nothing, waiting patiently, letting the silence stretch just long enough to prompt a response.

Grimal wasn't the type to spill details without a good reason, but silence often worked better than words. It gave people room to think, to fill the empty space with their own voices. I kept my expression neutral, my curiosity carefully masked behind a polite, almost detached demeanor.

"Barbara," he said finally, his tone heavy with warning. "Don't go sticking your nose where it doesn't belong."

"Me?" I asked, widening my eyes in mock innocence. "I'm just here waiting for my shrimp lo mein."

Grimal was a man who appreciated directness but only when it came with a side of subtlety. Too much prodding, and he'd shut down entirely.

Just then, May Lee appeared, carrying a brown paper bag with my order inside, her cheerful smile a welcome interruption. "Here you go, Barbara. Hot and ready," she said brightly, holding the bag out toward me.

"Perfect timing," I said warmly, rising from my chair with the same casual ease I'd maintained throughout the conversation. "Thanks, May Lee."

She nodded, already moving toward the next customer, her efficient energy a stark contrast to the deliberate pace of my conversation with Grimal. I turned back to him, flashing him another small, friendly smile. "Don't worry, Chief. I'll leave the detective work to you."

Grimal grunted in response, the sound somewhere between dismissal and acknowledgment.

As I adjusted the bag in my hand, I lingered by Grimal's table, feigning a casual air. "I did hear something interesting, though," I said as though the thought had just occurred to me, my tone light and conversational. "Cheerville TechXpo is quite the event, isn't it? A company like LuxTech being involved must mean big things for the town."

Grimal's gaze flicked up to meet mine, the wariness in his eyes unmistakable. He didn't say anything immediately, and I could almost see the gears turning in his head. "You're keeping up with tech news now?" he asked, his tone laced with mild suspicion, though not outright dismissive.

"Well, Pauline and Gretchen won't stop talking about it," I said with a soft laugh, letting the familiar names of the town's chatterboxes do some of the work for me. "Free smartwatches, chocolate fountains—it's all anyone can talk about." I paused, letting the statement hang in the air for a beat before continuing in a more thoughtful tone. "But personally, I'd think a company as big as LuxTech might need a little extra... oversight. Wouldn't you agree?"

Grimal's brow furrowed at that, the lines on his face deepening

"What's that supposed to mean?" he asked, his tone edged with suspicion.

I tilted my head slightly, my expression all innocence. "Nothing, Chief. Just that with everything going on lately, maybe it's worth keeping an eye on things. Big companies don't always have small-town interests at heart."

He leaned back in his chair, studying me with an expression that was equal parts annoyance and curiosity. "Barbara, if there's something you're not saying—"

"Oh, I'm saying everything," I interrupted

smoothly, flashing him another sweet, disarming smile. "Just making conversation."

He sighed heavily, his shoulders sagging even more as he rubbed the back of his neck. "Bryce's... heart attack," he began, his tone slower now, more deliberate. "There are some inconsistencies."

"Inconsistencies?" I echoed, keeping my voice light with just a hint of curiosity. My head tilted slightly, as though I were hearing this for the first time, though inside I was already piecing together what he might mean. "That sounds mysterious."

Grimal hesitated, his lips pressing into a thin line as he seemed to weigh the risks of letting me in on whatever he was holding back. His eyes narrowed slightly, scrutinizing me.

"You know me, Chief," I said with a small shrug. "Just trying to stay in the loop. You never know when a little information might help ease the town's gossip mill."

He let out a long breath, the reluctance in his body language evident. His gaze lingered on mine for a moment longer before he finally relented, his voice low as though trying to shield his words from prying ears. "Fine," he said at last, his tone carrying a note of resignation. "But this doesn't leave this conversation, got it?"

"Of course," I replied, nodding solemnly with just the right amount of sincerity. "You have my word."

Grimal leaned forward slightly, lowering his voice even further. "The toxicology report flagged something," he admitted, his tone heavy with both frustration and unease. "Trace amounts of a substance we couldn't identify. The lab's running more tests, but whatever it is, it's not something we've seen before."

"Something foreign, maybe?" I asked.

"Could be," he said, his brow furrowing deeply as he leaned back again, crossing his arms over his chest. "Or something new. Either way, it's raising red flags."

"And I suppose the timing doesn't help," I said, gesturing vaguely with one hand as though the thought were an afterthought. "With the tech expo coming up and all."

Grimal's expression darkened slightly, his lips pressing into another thin line. "Stay out of trouble, Barbara," he said, his tone firm but lacking real conviction.

"Always," I replied lightly, offering him one last disarming smile as I turned to leave.

As the bell jingled above me and the door swung

shut behind me, I let out a small breath I hadn't realized I'd been holding. Grimal's reluctance to share was typical, but the information he'd let slip was more than enough to confirm what I already suspected: Bryce Thornton had been poisoned.

My appetite was fading, replaced by a gnawing sense of urgency. Whatever was happening in Cheerville, time was running out, and I needed to act fast.

SEVEN

The Cheerville TechXpo was nothing short of a spectacle, a dizzying display of innovation and sensory overload that transformed the usually sleepy convention center into a hive of activity. Rows of sleek booths stretched the length of the hall, illuminated by vibrant LED panels, glowing holographic displays, and flashing screens that demanded attention from every angle. The hum of excited chatter mixed with the occasional mechanical whir of drones zipping overhead, their tiny rotors slicing through the air as they performed demonstrations for wide-eyed onlookers.

Salespeople, each more animated than the last, stood at their stations, extolling the virtues of their gadgets to anyone who paused long enough to listen. The words "revolutionary" and "cutting-edge" were tossed around like confetti, while enthusiastic crowds jostled to catch glimpses of virtual reality headsets, AI-powered assistants, and self-driving robots.

I wasn't here for the giveaways or the novelty of watching a robotic dog dance to pop music. My focus wasn't on the tech itself—it was on the people behind it. Somewhere among the sleek booths and flashing lights, I knew the cartel was lurking, weaving their plans into the fabric of this event. And it was up to me to stop them.

Of course, blending in was key. Today, I wasn't Barbara Gold, ex-CIA operative—I was an ordinary grandmother, curious about the marvels of modern technology. My floral blouse, wide-brimmed sunhat, and oversized tote bag brimming with pamphlets painted the perfect picture of a retiree eager to keep up with the times. A good spy knows how to disappear into the background, and today, I intended to be invisible.

I strolled through the aisles at a leisurely pace, my gaze darting from booth to booth while I maintained an air of cheerful curiosity. Occasionally, I stopped to examine a gadget or gadget-like object, my expressions alternating between awe and mild confusion.

"Isn't that clever?" I muttered, just loud enough for passersby to hear, as I snapped a photo of a robotic vacuum. I nodded approvingly at its smooth maneuvers, as if planning to regale my book club with tales of this wondrous cleaning innovation.

At one booth, a young salesperson enthusiastically demonstrated a smartwatch that could monitor hydration levels. "Perfect for those of us who forget to drink water," he said with a grin, his polished sales pitch landing somewhere between earnest and overly rehearsed.

I squinted at the watch, leaning closer with a look of exaggerated intrigue. "It even tells you *when* to drink? My goodness, what will they think of next?"

The young man beamed, clearly pleased with my reaction. I nodded once more, murmuring something about how impressed my grandson would be, before moving on. Behind the mask of curiosity, my mind was racing. Every smartwatch, every gadget, every flashy display felt like a potential threat, a puzzle piece that might fit into the bigger picture of Protocol 73.

As I wandered deeper into the expo, the crowd

thickened, and the energy in the room seemed to hum with a life of its own. Attendees huddled around demonstration tables, their faces lit with the glow of screens as they watched drones perform aerial acrobatics or tested the responsiveness of voice-controlled devices. The sheer scale of the event was overwhelming, but I forced myself to stay focused.

I stopped at another booth, this one showcasing a line of sleek virtual reality headsets. A small group had gathered to watch as a volunteer donned the headset, their movements clumsy as they reached for objects only they could see. I lingered at the edge of the crowd, pretending to be fascinated by the display while keeping an eye on the booth attendants. My gut told me that the cartel wouldn't be so obvious as to flaunt their involvement, but I wasn't taking any chances.

"You can experience anything," one of the booth workers was saying, gesturing expansively. "Travel the world, dive under the ocean, or even explore outer space—all from the comfort of your living room!"

"Outer space?" I murmured to myself, shaking my head as though the idea were too much to comprehend. I pulled out my phone and snapped another photo, muttering something about how technology had come a long way since the rotary phone.

Every now and then, I caught snippets of conversations that floated above the noise—a tech enthusiast gushing about a new AI breakthrough, a parent wondering aloud if their child could use the gadgets they bought, a booth worker trying to close a sale. The words washed over me like background music.

Amid the clamor of flashing screens and enthusiastic sales pitches, I spotted a familiar duo. Gretchen and Pauline stood by a booth showcasing wearable heart monitors, their contrasting figures immediately recognizable. Gretchen, leaning on her walker with a confidence that belied her reliance on it, was deep in conversation—or, rather, interrogation—with a young booth attendant. The poor man looked like he'd stumbled into the lion's den, his polished sales pitch faltering under her unrelenting questions.

"So, it can predict heart attacks?" Gretchen asked, narrowing her eyes at the small device displayed on the table. Her tone was skeptical, but the mischievous glint in her eye was unmistakable. "What about romance? Can it warn me when a handsome man is nearby?"

The attendant blinked, clearly caught off guard. "Uh... no, ma'am. It's, um, designed to monitor—"

"Oh, what a shame," Gretchen interrupted with a dramatic sigh, leaning more heavily on her walker. "I suppose I'll just have to rely on my own instincts for that."

Beside her, Pauline's mouth twitched as she suppressed a laugh. "If it could detect chocolate, I'd buy two," she quipped, her voice dripping with humor.

The attendant gave a nervous chuckle, glancing around as if searching for an escape route. I decided to intervene before Gretchen could press him further, making my way over with a smile.

"Having fun, I see," I said as I approached, my voice light enough to blend with the cheerful atmosphere.

Pauline turned, her face lighting up. "Barbara! They're raffling off smartwatches at the LuxTech booth. They're giving five away every hour! You should enter."

"And don't forget the chocolate fountain," Gretchen added conspiratorially, leaning in as if sharing a great secret. "It's near the snack area. Priorities, you know."

I laughed, the sound genuine despite the tension

simmering beneath my surface calm. "I'll keep that in mind," I said. "Just don't overdo it. This place is bigger than it looks, and I'd hate for you to wear yourselves out."

Pauline waved off my concern with a dismissive hand. "Nonsense. Gretchen and I have stamina," she declared. "Go enter that LuxTech raffle! A free smartwatch? How could you pass that up?"

I nodded, though the mention of the raffle sent a chill down my spine. Free smartwatches. The phrase echoed ominously in my mind, summoning the image of rows of unsuspecting attendees walking away with devices designed to betray them. LuxTech was dispersing weapons, though no one here would realize it until it was too late.

The thought of Pauline and Gretchen strapping one onto their wrists made my stomach turn.

The raffle would attract a crowd, and a crowd meant distraction—something I might be able to use.

"Well, don't wait too long," Pauline added. "The line's already huge!"

Gretchen resumed her questioning, turning her attention back to the beleaguered attendant. "What about this monitoring app you keep talking about?" she asked, tapping the table with her free hand. "Does it track everything? Because I don't need anyone spying on me when I'm eating my cookies at midnight."

Pauline chuckled, shaking her head. "Gretchen, I think you're supposed to wear it, not confess your sins to it."

"I just want to know what it's capable of," Gretchen said with a shrug, clearly enjoying herself.

The attendant stammered, attempting to explain the device's features without much success. I caught myself smiling. Watching the two of them in action, so vibrant and full of life, was a reminder of why I needed to succeed.

The LuxTech booth was impossible to miss. Its sleek, minimalist design stood out amidst the sensory overload of the expo. Spotlights framed the booth's rotating display of smartwatches, casting a subtle glow that drew attendees like moths to a flame. The company's latest wearable—a glossy, streamlined model with a bold tagline promising "Innovation on Your Wrist"—was the star of the show, and a steady stream of curious onlookers crowded around to get a closer look.

I lingered nearby, feigning interest in a pamphlet advertising "Next-Gen Fitness Tracking" while keeping my true focus elsewhere. My eyes scanned the booth, taking in every detail: the eager sales staff, the glossy brochures, the strategically placed demo units. It was a picture-perfect display of corporate marketing. I lingered at the booth for a while, then stood in line at the raffle as an excuse to continue keeping an eye on this area.

While waiting, my attention snagged on something—or rather, someone—just outside the action.

A man stood slightly apart from the crowd, his posture rigid and his movements too precise to be casual. He was dressed like a professional—sharp blazer, neatly combed hair—but there was an undercurrent of tension in the way his eyes darted around the room, scanning the sea of attendees with a careful, almost predatory air. Unlike the rest of the crowd, he wasn't engaging with the sales staff or gawking at the gadgets. He wasn't here to admire the technology. He was working.

I didn't know him, but I recognized his type. The way he carried himself, the way his gaze lingered just long enough to assess without drawing attention—it was a look I'd seen countless times in my former life. He was here for a purpose, and it wasn't to win a raffle or marvel at holographic displays.

My pulse quickened as I peeked beneath my sunhat and watched him slip a hand into his pocket, pulling out a small USB drive. The move was quick, practiced, and almost imperceptible—almost. My heart thudded as he glanced around, ensuring no one was watching too closely. But he hadn't accounted for me.

All the booth attendants were busy, their attention split between answering questions from a group of overly enthusiastic teenagers and managing the steady flow of visitors, and of course, managing the line for the raffle. It gave him just enough of a window to act.

With fluid efficiency, the man moved toward the smartwatch display. He bent down slightly, his movements precise but deliberately unremarkable, and plugged the USB drive into a hidden port at the back of the pedestal. The action took no more than a few seconds, but to me, it felt like an eternity. I held my breath, my grip tightening on the pamphlet in my hand as I resisted the urge to step forward.

He straightened quickly, brushing off his blazer with an air of nonchalance as if he'd done nothing out of the ordinary. His expression was carefully neutral, but the faint stiffness in his shoulders betrayed him. He took a step back, blending seamlessly into the crowd, and within moments, he was gone.

My heart still pounded as I replayed what I'd

just witnessed. The man's movements were subtle, designed to avoid suspicion, but they carried the unmistakable precision of someone trained for this kind of work.

I forced myself to stay put, then entered myself in for the raffle with a fake name and contact details. Then I got out of line and flipped through more pamphlets at the booth, pretending to read about the smartwatch's features, though the words barely registered.

The USB drive. This man wasn't just tampering with the devices—he was planting something. A program, perhaps, or a payload that would trigger at the right moment. Whatever it was, it wasn't good.

The crowd around me doubled and I seized the opportunity to move closer to the pedestal. My steps were deliberate, measured, blending into the flow of attendees as I approached it. From this angle, I could see the faint outline of the port the man had used, tucked neatly behind the rotating stand.

I glanced over my shoulder, scanning the crowd for any sign of him. He was gone—disappeared into the sea of expo-goers like a ghost. Only when I was sure he was gone did I make my move.

"Excuse me," I said, directing my attention to one of the booth attendants. A young woman with a cheerful smile and a LuxTech-branded lanyard turned to me eagerly. I gestured toward the smart-watch spinning slowly on its pedestal. "Does this one track steps and sleep?"

"Yes, ma'am!" she said brightly, clearly delighted to have an audience. "Not only does it track your steps and sleep, but it also monitors your heart rate, hydration levels, and even stress levels. It's one of the most advanced wearables on the market!"

As she launched into her polished sales pitch, her voice bubbling with enthusiasm, I feigned rapt attention, nodding occasionally as though hanging on her every word. "Oh, how fascinating," I murmured, keeping my tone light. "I could certainly use a gadget like that to keep me on track."

While she spoke, I shifted my tote bag higher on my shoulder, using the movement as cover to lean slightly toward the pedestal. My hand slipped behind the display, my fingers brushing against the small USB drive the man had inserted moments earlier. It was cool to the touch, no larger than my thumb, and I felt a slight prickle of nerves as I wrapped my fingers around it.

With a quick, practiced motion, I palmed the drive and slipped it into my pocket. My heart pounded, but outwardly, I remained calm, offering the attendant another polite nod as she continued her enthusiastic explanation.

"Thank you for your time," I said, cutting her off gently before she could delve into another feature. "This has been very enlightening. I'll have to think about it."

"Of course, ma'am!" she replied with a smile. "Let us know if you have any questions."

I stepped away from the booth, my expression serene as I adjusted the strap of my tote bag. Inside, however, my thoughts were anything but calm. The weight of the USB drive in my pocket was a tangible reminder of the stakes, and I resisted the urge to glance over my shoulder to see if anyone had noticed.

"Barbara!" Gretchen called, waving me over to another booth a few steps away. She and Pauline stood in front of a gleaming display showcasing a futuristic-looking gadget. From a distance, it looked like a souped-up coffee maker, but as I got closer, I realized it was something far stranger.

"Did you see this?" Pauline asked, her excitement palpable. "It's a self-cleaning blender! You just add water and soap, and it cleans itself. Isn't that clever?"

I forced a smile, nodding politely. "Very clever." My focus was anywhere but on the blender; my mind was already racing with plans to get home and decrypt the USB. But Pauline and Gretchen weren't ones to let me off the hook easily.

The attendant, a young woman with an overly enthusiastic grin, launched into a practiced sales pitch. "Not only does it clean itself, but it also connects to your smartphone! You can program recipes, set timers, and even get nutritional information for everything you make."

"Connects to your smartphone," I muttered, the phrase hitting a nerve. Another piece of technology feeding into the ever-growing web of connectivity—and potential vulnerabilities. "Does everything have to be connected these days?"

"Come on, Barbara," Gretchen said. "Don't be such a Luddite. You could use one of these for your smoothies."

"I'm more of a tea person," I replied, though my tone lacked its usual sharpness. My thoughts had already drifted back to the USB. LuxTech's smartwatches weren't just about convenience; they were weapons waiting to be activated. What if other devices at this expo were just as dangerous?

Pauline nudged me, pulling me back to the present. "You entered the raffle, right? Imagine if you win! A smartwatch and a self-cleaning blender. You'd be the queen of tech!"

I laughed lightly, masking the unease curling in my stomach. "I think I'd leave the tech crown to you, Pauline."

As the attendant continued her pitch, I caught myself glancing toward the exit. Every minute spent here felt like borrowed time. The USB in my pocket wasn't just a lead—it was the key to unraveling Protocol 73, and I needed to start analyzing it as soon as possible. Yet here I was, nodding along to a conversation about self-cleaning blenders while the clock ticked down.

"Barbara, what do you think?" Pauline asked, breaking into my thoughts.

I blinked. "About what?"

"About the blender!" Gretchen said, grinning. "You'd never have to scrub a smoothie cup again."

"Sounds revolutionary," I said dryly, earning a laugh from both women. "But I think I forgot to leave out food for Dandelion. I better go feed her."

"Are you coming back?" Pauline said. "There is still plenty of chocolate at the chocolate fountain!"

"Yes, I'll be back. Enjoy yourselves!" I said, waving them off as I headed out.

The cool late afternoon air hit my face as I

stepped outside to the parking lot. After I slide into the driver's seat, I locked the doors and took a steadying breath. I finally had the chance to uncover the truth.

"Let's see what you've got," I murmured, starting the engine. Whatever was on the USB, I was ready to face it.

EIGHT

Back home, the USB drive from LuxTech's booth sat on my dining table like a ticking time bomb. The small, metallic device gleamed faintly under the dining room light, a stark contrast to the dark implications it carried. I wondered how many people had already walked away from the expo with one of them, completely unaware of the danger they'd taken home.

Dandelion perched on the table beside the USB, her tail flicking absently over the scattered notes I'd hastily jotted down earlier. The soft rustle of paper seemed to echo in the quiet room, a faint reminder of how much was at stake. She let out a soft meow, her green eyes narrowing at the tiny device as though she could sense the malevolence hidden within its sleek design. For a moment, it almost seemed like she was daring it to make a move.

"Not for you, girl," I murmured, reaching out to scratch her head. My fingertips brushed against her soft fur, and the steady rhythm of her purring filled the air, grounding me in a way that nothing else could. Her calm, unbothered demeanor stood in stark contrast to the unease bubbling beneath my skin. I took a deep breath, letting the sound of her purring steady my nerves before turning my attention back to the laptop. "Let's see what you're hiding."

Sliding the USB into my laptop port, I felt a pang of unease as the faint chime confirmed the connection. It was a small, innocuous sound, yet it sent a ripple of tension through me. The screen flickered to life, displaying a single folder labeled "P73_Deployer." Its bluntness leaving no room for ambiguity. This wasn't a collection of harmless marketing files or flashy promotional material—it was something far darker.

With a click, the folder opened, and my unease deepened as a list of files appeared on the screen: "Activation_Protocol," "Deploy_Logs," "Target_Map," and "Field_Test_Results." Each name felt more ominous than the last, a breadcrumb trail leading straight to the heart of LuxTech's sinister agenda. My fingers hovered over the trackpad, hesitation creeping in as I considered my options. The activation protocol seemed like the obvious place to start, but I couldn't shake the feeling that opening it might trigger something unintended. A trap, perhaps. Or worse.

I opted for caution, choosing instead to start with the "Deploy_Logs." The screen filled with rows of data, a sea of information that took a moment to parse. Timestamps, device IDs, and connection statuses scrolled across the screen in neat, clinical lines. Each entry represented one of the smart-watches about to be handed out at the expo, every single one marked as "ready." My chest tightened as I scrolled through the list, the weight of what this meant pressing down on me like a physical force. Dozens of devices, all primed for activation. This was a bigger test run, a live operation, waiting for the right moment to go into effect.

A small notification in the corner of the log caught my attention: "System Sync Complete. Countdown Active." The words seemed to pulse on the screen, their significance hitting me like a punch to the gut. I stared at the notification, my mind racing to comprehend the implications. A countdown. How long? What was the target? The questions swirled in my head, each more urgent than the last.

My pulse quickened as I navigated back to the main folder and clicked on "Activation_Protocol." The screen went dark for a moment, a chilling pause that felt like the calm before the storm. When it came back to life, the sight before me sent a fresh wave of dread coursing through my veins: a live countdown, its stark white numbers ticking down against a black background.

"4 hours, 12 minutes remaining."

The sight of it held me frozen for a moment, my mind reeling. Each second that passed brought the operation closer to fruition, and I had no way of knowing what would happen when the timer hit zero. My fingers hovered over the keyboard, itching to take action, but the enormity of the situation left me momentarily paralyzed. I glanced at Dandelion, her serene expression a stark contrast to the storm of emotions swirling within me. Her tail flicked once more, brushing against my scattered notes as if urging me to keep moving.

The room felt colder, the quiet heavier, as though the ticking countdown had somehow sucked the warmth and air from the space. My chest tightened further as I forced myself to focus, my mind racing through possible next steps. The clock was ticking, and whatever LuxTech had planned was set to unfold in just over four hours, at exactly 10pm. The question was no longer whether I could stop it but how—and if I could do it in time.

I clicked into the "Field_Test_Results" file, desperate to understand the full scope of Protocol 73. The report detailed a series of experiments conducted in controlled environments. Each test documented the smartwatch's effects on its wearer:

• **Subject 1:** Device triggered false emergency alerts, sending a flood of fake distress calls to local authorities.

• **Subject 2:** Wearer's personal data was harvested and sent to an encrypted server, leaving their financial accounts vulnerable to exploitation.

• **Subject 3:** Heart rate monitors were manipulated to induce panic, leading to symptoms mimicking a medical emergency.

The tests varied, but the outcome was always the same: chaos.

Navigating back to the "Target_Map," I pulled up a heatmap of Cheerville. Red dots lit up across the town, clustering around the expo hall and spilling into nearby neighborhoods. A single line of text beneath the map read: "Phase 1: Local Deployment. Phase 2: Regional Expansion."

The simplicity of the plan was chilling. The cartel wasn't just testing Protocol 73—they were scaling it. If they wanted mass destruction, that would be possible in the future if they succeeded in their tests. Once Cheerville proved the system's effectiveness, they would unleash it on larger populations, turning LuxTech's reputation into a Trojan horse.

The countdown on the screen ticked down relentlessly: 4 hours, 7 minutes. The numbers glowed an ominous red. Beneath the countdown was a single line of text: "Deployment Radius: 50 miles. Activation Mode: Adaptive."

My breath caught. Adaptive. The smartwatches weren't just infected—they were personalized weapons. Each device would pull from its wearer's synced data to determine how best to cause disruption. For one person, it might send fake medical alerts; for another, it could trigger financial sabotage. The variability was deliberate, designed to spread chaos and confusion. Cheerville's residents were guinea pigs to test out what the cartel could do.

The USB's purpose was clear now: to infect all connected devices and activate Protocol 73. And its activation was already successful. The smartwatches, being raffled off and handed out like party favors, weren't just promotional gadgets—they were ticking time bombs, their dormant malware waiting for this drive to set them into motion.

At the bottom of the "Activation_Protocol" file, the same small symbol caught my eye: a triangle intersected by a diagonal line. That symbol. A signature as clear as a fingerprint.

Dandelion stretched across the table, her paw nudging my notebook as though urging me to act. "You're right," I said softly, rubbing her head. "We don't have time to second-guess."

The countdown continued to tick, each passing second bringing Cheerville inexorably closer to disaster. On the surface, the town carried on as usual —quiet streets, porch lights glowing, and the faint hum of evening routines—but I knew the truth. At 10 p.m., every infected smartwatch would execute its commands, transforming this idyllic town into ground zero for the cartel's twisted ambitions. The thought sent a chill through me.

My first instinct was to call Grimal. A case this large, this urgent, demanded his attention. But I knew how that conversation would go—questions, demands for proof, an inevitable delay while he tried to wrap his head around the enormity of what I was saying. Time wasn't on my side, and explaining all this to him would take more time than I could afford. If I wanted to stop this, I'd have to act alone. There was no room for hesitation.

I stood, the decision firm in my mind. Dandelion let out a soft trill from her perch on the table, her bright green eyes following my every move with feline curiosity. Her purring filled the quiet room, a steady reminder of the calm I needed to carry with me. "I've got work to do. We're going to be here a while." She nuzzled my hand briefly, her way of giving silent encouragement, before resettling herself on the table.

It had been years since I'd last worked with high-level encryption, but as I returned to the laptop and reopened the files, it felt like no time had passed. The instincts came flooding back, sharp and intact. The knowledge, the discipline, the ability to find patterns hidden in chaos—it all clicked into place as though I'd never stopped. The cartel had buried their secrets beneath layers of complexity, creating barriers meant to repel even the most seasoned intruder. But I wasn't here to be repelled. I was here to break through.

There's always a way in. You just have to know where to look.

My fingers moved across the keyboard with practiced precision, the soft clicks creating a steady rhythm that matched the hum of the laptop fan. The files weren't just encrypted; they were intricately linked, feeding into a central system designed to sync across multiple devices. This wasn't just a clever bit of programming—it was a network, meticulously crafted and terrifyingly efficient. The smartwatches weren't standalone units, as they had been marketed. They were nodes in a web, each one tethered to a primary server that held the reins. If I could map that network, chart its connections and vulnerabilities, I might be able to do more than just stop the system. I might be able to turn it against itself.

I leaned closer to the screen, my pulse steady despite the enormity of the task before me. The logs were dense with information. Beneath the logs, a new set of variables caught my eye. They were simple in appearance—controls labeled for activation, override, and reset functions. Yet their implications were profound. These weren't locked commands. There were no safeguards in place. They were accessible, waiting for someone to act. The realization hit me like a jolt of electricity: the cartel hadn't just built a weapon; they'd left it armed and dangerously exposed.

I let out a slow breath, forcing myself to remain calm. The path forward was clear, but the stakes had never been higher. Each second brought the count-down closer to zero, closer to a moment that would change everything. My mind raced through possibili-ties, calculating risks and outcomes. The controls were there, waiting to be used. As my fingers hovered over the keyboard, I knew this was my chance.

"Interesting," I murmured under my breath, my mind racing as I began copying fragments of the code into a separate file. The lines of data scrolled endlessly across the screen, intricate and layered, a testament to the sophistication of the system the cartel had built to execute Protocol 73. It was impressive, no doubt, but its very complexity was also a glaring vulnerability. Networks like this, no matter how elaborate, were only as strong as their foundation. Overload the system, disrupt its signals, and the entire structure could collapse like a house of cards.

But identifying a weakness wasn't the same as exploiting it. To do that, I'd need to build something of my own—a countermeasure strong enough to topple what they'd constructed. My fingers began moving faster. The rhythm of the keys beneath my fingertips was both familiar and urgent, like slipping back into an old skillset I hadn't realized I still carried. I wasn't just sifting through data anymore; I was creating something new, constructing a response designed to turn their weapon against them.

The feedback loop wasn't fully formed yet, but the framework was taking shape on the screen in front of me. Each line of code brought me closer to an algorithm capable of intercepting and corrupting the commands being sent to the smartwatches. If I could finish it in time, the devices wouldn't just fail to execute Protocol 73—they'd shut the entire network down in the process. It was a bold move, but boldness had served me well in the past.

Of course, it wasn't without risk. A countermeasure like this wouldn't go unnoticed for long. Whoever was monitoring the system would know the instant their network faltered. The alarms would go off, figuratively or maybe even literally. But if the feedback loop worked as intended, it wouldn't matter. By the time they realized what was happening, it would already be too late. The system would be in chaos, and their control would be gone.

The countdown on the screen ticked on relentlessly, the numbers flashing in steady rhythm: "3 hours, 17 minutes remaining." Each second felt like it slipped through my fingers, a constant reminder that I was working against the clock. The temptation to rush was overwhelming, but I knew better. This wasn't something that could be hurried. Every line of code had to be precise, every piece of the loop calibrated with exacting care. One mistake could have disastrous consequences—triggering the system prematurely or, worse, strengthening it instead of dismantling it.

From the corner of my eye, I caught Dandelion's small, watchful figure. She let out a soft trill, her green eyes fixed on me as though sensing the weight of the moment. She stretched slightly, her paw brushing against the edge of my notebook, as if urging me to stay focused. "I know, girl," I murmured, reaching out to scratch her head absently. The steady rhythm of her purring brought a fleeting sense of calm, grounding me as I returned my attention to the screen. "This has to work."

I paused, my gaze scanning the variables again, looking for anything I might have missed. A few lines of code stood out, their purpose cryptic but clearly critical. Adjusting them felt like twisting a lockpick inside a stubborn mechanism, each tiny adjustment bringing the system closer to collapse. Slowly, carefully, I tweaked the parameters, testing each change before moving to the next. The tension was palpable, each keystroke carrying the weight of potential success—or failure.

By the time I leaned back in my chair, the ache in my shoulders was almost unbearable, and my eyes burned from the strain of staring at the screen for so long. The feedback loop wasn't active yet, but the foundation was solid, hidden within the system like a dormant seed waiting to sprout. When the moment came, I'd be ready to deploy it with a single command.

Dandelion stretched across the table again, her paw nudging my notebook as though reminding me of the ticking clock. Her movements were calm, unhurried, but the gesture served its purpose, drawing my attention back to the urgency of the situation. I glanced at the countdown, the numbers glaring back at me: "0 hours, 47 minutes remaining." The time was slipping away faster now, each moment pulling me closer to the point of no return.

The air in the room felt heavier, charged with anticipation. I allowed myself one deep breath, steadying the surge of adrenaline threatening to cloud my judgment. The task ahead was clear, but the stakes had never been higher.

NINE

The Cheerville TechXpo, vibrant and buzzing during the day, was winding down as the clock neared 10:00 p.m. The once-crowded aisles, alive with flashing holographic displays and enthusiastic sales pitches, were now quieting as exhibitors packed up their gear and attendees trickled toward the exits. Overhead speakers crackled intermittently, urging stragglers to "make their way to the doors—thank you for attending!"

I lingered near the LuxTech booth, careful to stay inconspicuous as I pretended to examine a nearby display touting "The Smart Kitchen of Tomorrow." Its glossy surfaces and sleek appliances were the perfect cover for my watchful gaze. Vendors were focused on their own stations, dismantling displays and loading equipment into branded cases. Even the occasional security guard barely spared me a glance. As far as they were concerned, I was just another harmless attendee soaking up the last moments of tech splendor.

But I wasn't here to marvel at connected blenders or self-stocking fridges. My focus remained on LuxTech, the epicenter of the cartel's plan, and the gleaming smartwatches still displayed on their pristine pedestals. Their smooth, polished exteriors masked the danger they carried—a danger I couldn't allow to be unleashed.

As the speakers announced the expo's official closure, I slipped away from the kitchen display, moving deliberately but casually toward a darker corner near LuxTech's sprawling setup. A VR gaming company's booth loomed nearby, its over-sized monitors and partially disassembled demo stations offering the perfect cover. The deactivated lights cast long shadows, and the maze of equipment screens provided just enough obstruction to obscure me from view.

Crouching low, I adjusted my position until I had a clear line of sight to the LuxTech booth. From here, the smartwatches gleamed faintly under the dim overhead lights. Even in the quiet stillness of the nearly empty expo hall, they seemed to hum with potential—an eerie reminder of what they were designed to do.

Movement near the booth caught my eye, and my breath hitched. A man in a tailored blazer stepped into view, his posture confident but his darting gaze giving him away. It was the same man I'd seen earlier at the LuxTech display—the one who had planted the USB at the pedestal. His deliberate movements then had set my instincts humming, and now, seeing him again, those instincts screamed confirmation.

I stiffened, keeping perfectly still as he pulled a sleek tablet from his pocket and began tapping its screen. His expression was sharp, his movements deliberate. This wasn't someone casually packing up after a long day—this was someone ensuring that everything was running as planned.

The cartel wasn't careless. They wouldn't leave a scheme like this on autopilot. Protocol 73 might have been programmed to activate at 10 p.m., but if something went wrong—if the system lagged or if someone interfered—they'd want someone on-site to ensure it worked. This man wasn't just a technician; he was a monitor, a failsafe.

The tablet glowed faintly as he swiped through

screens, pausing occasionally to glance at the smart-watches on the pedestals. Whatever he was looking at wasn't visible to anyone without his access. From my vantage point, I could only guess, but his confident posture suggested everything was proceeding according to plan.

The LuxTech booth remained as pristine as ever, the smartwatches glowing faintly in the dim light. Their unassuming appearance only made them more dangerous—silent weapons lying in wait. I knew they were already infected, primed to activate in just ten minutes.

I stayed crouched, my breath steady as I watched him. Every instinct in my body screamed caution—this wasn't just any LuxTech employee. His deliberate movements, his intense focus on the tablet, and the calculated way he scanned the booth marked him as something more. Cartel, through and through.

And he was in my way.

The USB drive in my pocket felt heavier with every passing second, a reminder of what I had to do. My earlier work on the laptop wasn't finished; the feedback loop I'd designed was ready to deploy, but I needed access to LuxTech's central hub—the very system this man was monitoring. Without it, the loop was just a theory, a plan scribbled in code with no way to execute it.

The LuxTech booth was the nerve center. To disrupt Protocol 73, I had to upload my countermeasure directly into the system. And that meant getting to the pedestal he was guarding.

My mind raced as I watched him, my fingers tightening around the edge of the booth I was hiding behind. If he stayed there, my entire plan would fall apart. I couldn't risk sneaking past him—not with the countdown ticking relentlessly toward 10 p.m. and every second bringing us closer to chaos. The devices needed to be deactivated now, not after the cartel's plan went live.

As the last of the security guards began their sweeps, I slipped deeper into the shadows, ensuring I wouldn't be seen. This wasn't the moment to act boldly—it was the moment to prepare.

The lights in the expo hall were already dimmed to signal closing time, but enough illumination remained to cast unwanted clarity on my every movement. If I wanted access to the LuxTech booth without drawing attention, I'd need more cover—preferably in the form of darkness.

Find the light switch, create a distraction, and slip in undetected. The plan was simple, and while it carried its risks, it was my best shot. Moving cautiously, I edged toward the wall near the front doors, where I suspected the controls for the hall's lighting might be hidden. My pulse quickened as I scanned the area, keeping my steps deliberate and quiet. The sound of my own breathing seemed louder than it should have been.

But just as I neared the wall, the creak of wheels on the polished floor froze me in place.

"Barbara," Gretchen appeared from around the corner or a booth, her walker's reflective strips glowing faintly in the dim light. Her expression was equal parts cheerful and determined, as though this were a casual shopping trip and not the closing moments of a covert operation.

I straightened, forcing a calm smile. "Gretchen, what are you doing here?" I asked, keeping my tone light despite the tension thrumming through me.

"I was just checking to see if they left any of that chocolate fountain behind. You wouldn't believe the amount they wasted earlier. It was practically a crime." Gretchen said. "Pauline's outside with the chocolates, we can give you some! We have plenty. What are you doing back here? And... what's with the outfit? All black?"

I straightened, forcing a casual laugh. "Gretchen,

it's just practical. Black doesn't show stains or wrinkles, and it's comfortable. Besides, I didn't exactly plan to make a fashion statement tonight."

She squinted at me, clearly unconvinced. "You're usually in something colorful. I don't think I've ever seen you dressed like this, Barbara. Are you sure you're feeling all right?"

"Perfectly fine," I replied breezily, brushing imaginary dust off my sleeve. "This is just what I threw on before heading out. You know how these expos are—lots of walking, lots of crowds. I wanted to keep it simple."

Her gaze lingered, her curiosity evident. "Hmm. Well, it's very... sleek."

"I'll take that as a compliment," I said with a faint smile, steering the conversation back on track. "Now, why are you still here? The lights are about to go out soon—it could get hazardous."

Her eyes widened slightly, the concern in her gaze replacing her earlier curiosity. "The lights are going out? Why didn't anyone say anything? That sounds dangerous!"

I nodded solemnly, leaning into her worry. "Exactly why you should head out. It's already getting darker, and I don't want you tripping over something." I gestured toward the exit. "Pauline's probably waiting for you. Why don't you find her, and I'll meet you both outside in a few minutes? I just need to pick something up from one of the vendors."

"She's at the health monitor booth," Gretchen grumbled as she shuffled away. "I told her I'd be right back, but you know how she gets when I take too long."

"Exactly why you should hurry," I said, my voice warm but insistent. "Go. I'll meet you both outside in a few minutes."

"Fine, fine," she said, waving me off with an exaggerated motion. "But don't dawdle, Barbara. And don't trip over any of those cables you're so worried about."

I watched her go, exhaling, letting the tension bleed out of my shoulders. Gretchen meant well, but her timing was as impeccable as a rainstorm on laundry day.

Refocusing, I turned my attention back to the LuxTech booth. The cartel operative was still stationed there, his tablet glowing faintly as he scrolled through whatever data he was monitoring. His posture remained sharp, his movements deliberate. He wasn't going anywhere.

I slipped further into the shadows, my gaze

darting toward the wall where I'd spotted the light switches earlier. If I could cut the remaining lights, I'd have a clear shot at the pedestal without drawing attention to myself.

Moving silently, I made my way to the switches, keeping my steps deliberate and controlled. The hall was eerily quiet, the faint hum of electronics the only sound. Every few seconds, I glanced over my shoulder, ensuring no one else had entered the area. The last thing I needed was another interruption.

The light switches were exactly where I'd expected them to be: a small panel set into the wall, partially hidden behind a stack of crates labeled "Demo Equipment—Fragile." I crouched down, flipping open the panel to reveal a series of labeled toggles.

"Main Hall Lighting" was printed neatly beside one of the switches. Perfect.

I hesitated for a moment, my hand hovering over the switch. Turning off the lights would give me the cover I needed, but it would also alert the operative that something was wrong. I'd have to move fast—very fast.

Taking a deep breath, I flicked the switch. The hall plunged into near-total darkness, the faint glow from a few scattered screens the only remaining light source.

I lingered in the shadows for a moment, waiting for my eyes to adjust to the sudden darkness. The glow of scattered screens and emergency lights painted the hall in faint, ghostly hues. My gaze darted back toward the LuxTech booth, where the cartel operative had been stationed moments earlier. I didn't see him. He must've gone to see about the lighting issues, exactly like I wanted.

I didn't waste a second. With the lights out, I pulled out my black hat from my back pocket, put it on, and moved swiftly and silently toward the LuxTech booth. My heart pounded as I closed the distance, my fingers already brushing the USB drive in my pocket. The feedback loop I'd designed was ready, but I'd have to upload it quickly before the operative could figure out what was happening.

Reaching the pedestal, I crouched low, using the darkness as my shield. The smartwatches glowed faintly, their polished surfaces reflecting the faint light of the operative's tablet as he moved around the booth. Every instinct screamed at me to hurry, but I forced myself to stay calm and deliberate. This had to work.

Sliding the USB into the hidden port at the base

of the pedestal, I tapped a small sequence into the screen. The feedback loop began to upload, the progress bar crawling across the screen. My breath hitched as I watched it, every second stretching into an eternity.

The progress bar reached 50% when a faint sound behind me made my blood run cold—a soft click, like the heel of a shoe against the floor.

I froze, my body tense as I strained to hear. The hall was too quiet, the darkness pressing in on all sides. Was it the operative? Had he returned, or was someone else moving through the shadows?

I glanced at the progress bar—68%. Not fast enough.

Keeping my movements deliberate, I adjusted my position to minimize my silhouette against the faint light of the display. The smartwatches hummed softly as the upload continued, their glow casting faint reflections on the floor. The seconds stretched endlessly, each one marked by the slow advance of the progress bar.

At 97%, I heard it again—the faint sound of movement, closer this time. My pulse quickened, but I didn't dare turn around. The bar blinked "Complete" just as the sound stopped entirely, leaving an eerie silence in its wake.

I removed the USB drive, slipping it back into my pocket with practiced precision. The loop was live now, disrupting the activation signals embedded in the smartwatches. The devices were no longer the cartel's tools—they were neutralized. But I wasn't safe yet.

Crouching low, I edged away from the pedestal, keeping to the shadows as I scanned the area for signs of the operative. The thought of his disappearance lingered, unsettling and unresolved. Wherever he was, he wasn't finished. And neither was I.

The sound of heavy footsteps broke through the quiet hall, reverberating off the walls like a slow drumbeat. My stomach tightened, the progress I'd made with the feedback loop feeling suddenly fragile.

"Barbara Gold, what the hell are you doing here?"

I froze mid-step. Slowly, I turned to see Chief Grimal stomping toward me, his flashlight beam slicing through the dim light. His expression was a familiar mix of irritation and suspicion, though this time, his presence carried an extra weight of authority.

I breathed in relief to see him, and I emerged, and waved him over.

"Barbara Gold, what the hell are you doing here?"

I shushed him, and waved him to my hiding place.

"You're not supposed to meddle," he continued.

Grimal's flashlight swept over the LuxTech booth, landing on the pedestal where the smartwatches still gleamed faintly. For a moment, he said nothing, his frown deepening as he processed the scene

"Be quiet," I whispered. "And turn off your flashlight."

"What's your interest in this booth?" he asked, his tone less confrontational now, though no less probing.

"This is not the time for questions. He'll be back at any second."

"Who will be back? You shouldn't be here, Barbara. The expo's closed. Go home."

The hall suddenly buzzed with a low hum as the overhead lights flickered back to life, illuminating the space in a harsh, sterile glow. The shadows that had concealed me melted away, and my heart sank.

Grimal looked up sharply, his flashlight beam dimming against the flood of light. "What the hell?"

he muttered, glancing toward the now-brightly lit LuxTech booth.

The sound of hurried footsteps reached my ears before I saw him—the man from earlier, the cartel operative, running back toward the booth. His sharp blazer flared slightly as he skidded to a halt, his gaze snapping between me, Grimal, and the pedestal.

The tension in the room crackled like static electricity.

The man's jaw tightened as his eyes locked onto mine. His sharp features, already marked by suspicion, hardened further as he spotted Grimal standing beside the pedestal.

"Who are you?" he demanded, his tone cold and clipped. His accent was faint but distinct, betraying roots far from Cheerville.

Grimal stepped forward, his presence radiating authority. "Chief Grimal, Cheerville Police. And you are?"

The man's eyes flicked to the pedestal, his sharp mind likely piecing together that something had changed. The devices on display seemed untouched, but I knew he could sense that the balance had shifted.

Grimal crossed his arms, his scowl deepening.

"This is a closed expo. If you're not a vendor or an exhibitor, you need to leave."

The man's eyes darted between the pedestal and Grimal, his jaw tightening as though he were calculating his next move. His sharp gaze returned to me, lingering for a fraction longer than I liked. Whatever he suspected, I could see it gnawing at him.

"I do work here," the man said finally, his tone measured but strained. "I was just checking on the booth." His voice carried an edge that didn't match his polite words.

Grimal didn't budge. "Checking on what, exactly? The event's over."

The man smiled faintly, but it didn't reach his eyes. "I'm responsible for this booth. I'm closing down. LuxTech takes security very seriously."

"Then you won't mind answering a few questions," Grimal replied, stepping forward slightly. His hand hovered near his radio, and I could tell he was preparing to escalate this if the man didn't cooperate.

I checked my watch. It had just turned 10:00pm.

The man's eyes darted to his tablet on the pedestal. Then he checked the screen attached to the pedestals. He swiped quickly across one screen and the other, his motions precise but increasingly frantic. A frown etched deeper lines into his face as his jaw tightened. "No," he muttered under his breath, his voice barely audible. "That's not possible."

I tilted my head slightly, feigning innocence. "Something wrong?" I asked, my tone as casual as I could manage.

The man's glare snapped to me, his expression colder than ever. "What did you do?"

Grimal stepped between us, his voice sharp. "Back off. I don't know what's going on here, but I suggest you start explaining yourself before this gets worse."

The man ignored him, his focus entirely on me. "You've tampered with something. I know it."

I raised an eyebrow, crossing my arms in mock offense. "Me? Tamper? I'm just a curious retiree taking a stroll through the expo."

Grimal, clearly irritated, jabbed a finger toward the exit. "Enough. You're done here. Either explain yourself now, or I'll have you escorted out."

The man's body tensed, his fists clenching at his sides. He was trapped, and he knew it. But instead of responding, he turned back to the tablet, his fingers flying over the screen in one last desperate attempt to salvage whatever had failed.

It was too late.

"You've done something," he muttered, his voice

low but seething with anger. His grip on the tablet tightened as though he wanted to crush it. Then, without warning, he pivoted sharply and bolted toward the nearest exit.

"Hey!" Grimal barked, his voice echoing through the hall. He moved to give chase, but the man was fast, weaving through the maze of empty booths with alarming agility.

"He's running away!" I shouted, already in pursuit. My legs moved instinctively, the adrenaline firing me forward as I followed the sharp sound of his footsteps. Grimal was close behind, his heavy boots pounding against the polished floor.

Just as I rounded a corner, the entire expo plunged into darkness. An expo employee must've turned it off for real now that the expo was officially closed.

TEN

The expo hall was a maze of shadows and empty booths. My eyes stayed locked on the man ahead of me as he bolted toward the front doors. His sharp footsteps echoed relentlessly, a staccato rhythm of desperation. Behind me, Grimal's frustrated grunts and heavy footsteps trailed far behind, a clear reminder that cardio wasn't part of his routine.

"Barbara!" Grimal's voice rang out, his tone a mixture of exasperation and desperation, cutting through the echoing hall. "Stop! Don't do anything stupid!"

"Too late for that!" I shot back over my shoulder, my focus unwavering as I kept my sights on the operative's retreating figure. His movements were quick, but desperation had a way of making people careless. Every misstep, every rushed decision, played directly into my hands. I had years of experience turning panic into an advantage, and this time would be no different.

The man darted toward the front doors with a singular focus, his form illuminated briefly by the faint glow of emergency lights near the exit. His speed was impressive, but his movements betrayed his lack of strategy—he was running purely on adrenaline. As I followed, my gaze caught on a nearby booth, one I'd noted earlier as a display for cutting-edge fitness bands and resistance training gear. The sleek equipment was meant to symbolize strength and endurance, but to me, it was an opportunity.

My hand shot out instinctively, grabbing a length of thick, elastic tubing from the display. The material was sturdy, its stretch designed to withstand the strain of intense workouts. It wasn't exactly field-grade equipment, but I wasn't in a position to be picky. It would have to do.

The man reached the front doors, his hand slamming against the push bar with a metallic clang that reverberated through the space. He shoved with all his weight, clearly intent on escape. But before he could get the door open, I launched myself toward him, the tubing stretched taut between my hands like a makeshift garrote. Every muscle in my body tensed as I closed the gap between us, moving with the speed and precision of someone who had done this too many times to count.

The element of surprise was firmly on my side—he didn't even hear me coming. His focus was entirely on the door, on escape, and that was his fatal mistake. With a swift motion, I looped the tubing around his torso, pulling it tight as I twisted sharply to knock him off balance. The move was fluid, instinctual, a reflex honed by years of fieldwork. He stumbled, his arms flailing wildly as he struggled to grab the doorframe for support. His fingers brushed the edge, but it was too late.

With a sharp tug, I yanked him backward, using his own momentum against him. The force sent us both crashing to the ground in an ungraceful heap. The impact jolted through my body, a burst of pain radiating from my left arm as it broke my fall. I gritted my teeth against the ache, shoving it to the back of my mind. There was no time to dwell on pain—not when the stakes were this high.

Ignoring the sharp throb in my forearm, I moved

quickly to secure him. My hands worked with practiced efficiency, wrapping the tubing around his arms
as he thrashed beneath me. His struggles were strong
but uncoordinated, driven more by panic than
purpose. I tightened the loops with a series of precise
knots, my fingers moving as if on autopilot. The
elastic material stretched and flexed with his movements but held firm, a testament to its durability. His
attempts to free himself grew more frantic, but the
more he struggled, the tighter the bindings became.

The man let out a string of muffled curses,
twisting and writhing in a desperate bid for freedom.
I shifted my weight to keep him pinned, my knee
pressing into his back to limit his movements. Every
second mattered, every knot had to hold. My breath
came in steady bursts, the adrenaline coursing
through me keeping my focus razor-sharp.

The hall seemed to close in around us, the
shadows and silence amplifying the intensity of the
moment. The man's resistance began to wane, his
movements slowing as the futility of his situation set
in. But I didn't let my guard down—not yet. The
cartel didn't hire amateurs, and I wasn't about to be
caught off guard.

"Get off me!" he snarled, his voice rough with
rage and desperation, the sound echoing in the

cavernous space of the expo hall. His body twisted violently, muscles straining against the makeshift restraints in a futile attempt to break free. Every movement only served to tighten the tubing further, its design, meant to resist powerful forces, ironically perfect for immobilizing a grown man.

"You picked the wrong town," I said between labored breaths, securing the final knot with a sharp tug. The elastic material creaked under the strain, holding firm as the man let out another frustrated growl. Planting my knee firmly on his back, I added, "And the wrong grandmother."

His body tensed beneath me, another attempt to buck me off, but his strength was waning. The tubing held fast, and I shifted my weight to maintain control, the adrenaline coursing through me keeping the pain in my arm at bay. Each second felt stretched, every sound amplified—the faint hum of the lights above, the distant creak of the building settling, and the pounding of my own heartbeat in my ears.

It was then that Grimal finally stumbled into view, his heavy footsteps announcing his arrival before he came into focus. His face was flushed a deep red, beads of sweat glistening on his forehead as he struggled to catch his breath. Planting his hands on his knees, he bent forward, glaring at me with an expression that could only be described as incredulous fury, as though I were personally responsible for his lack of cardio.

"What... in the hell... are you doing?" he gasped, his voice sharp and uneven despite his exhaustion. His chest heaved with each breath, the effort of chasing us clearly taking its toll.

I straightened, stepping back from the operative and dusting off my jacket with deliberate nonchalance, as though this were an everyday occurrence. "Taking care of business, Chief," I replied smoothly, letting a hint of amusement slip into my tone. "You're welcome, by the way."

Grimal straightened slowly, his scowl deepening as he took in the scene before him. His eyes moved from the operative tied up with fitness tubing, still squirming against the restraints with an expression of frustration and barely contained rage, and back to me, standing there like nothing was out of the ordinary.

"Backup's on the way," he muttered. He shot me a glare so sharp it could have curdled milk, the corners of his mouth pulled down in a deep frown. It was the look of a man who knew he should be in control of the situation but wasn't.

The distant wail of sirens pierced the night, the sound growing steadily louder as it approached. The flashing red and blue lights of the patrol cars spilled into the hall, painting the windows at the front with streaks of color that danced across the walls. The sight and sound sent a rush of relief through me— backup meant I could slip away without raising too many eyebrows.

I bent down, adjusting the brim of my hat, which had done such a fine job of keeping me inconspicuous up until now. The movement was deliberate, a final touch to maintain the air of composure I'd worked so hard to project. "Looks like your reinforcements are here, Chief," I said lightly, gesturing toward the flashing lights that painted his face in alternating hues of red and blue. "I think this is my cue to leave."

Grimal's glare didn't falter, his lips pressing into a thin, disapproving line. He opened his mouth as if to argue, then thought better of it, shaking his head instead. The sound of car doors slamming and hurried footsteps approaching filled the air, the officers' shadows stretching long and distorted as they neared the entrance. I didn't wait for Grimal's response. The moment he turned to address his incoming team, I slipped into the shadows, my exit as quiet as it was calculated.

Grimal's scowl deepened, his expression a storm of frustration and authority. "You're not going anywhere. I need a full statement—"

"Of course, of course." My tone was calm, almost reassuring, as though I were completely on board with his demands. "But you've got things under control now, and I'm sure you'd rather I stay out of the way while you... do your thing."

I didn't give him a chance to argue. Without waiting for a response, I stepped back, pivoting on my heel as though this were the most natural conclusion to our conversation. My movements were deliberate but unhurried, projecting the confidence of someone who had nothing to hide. The side exit wasn't far, and I could already hear the faint voices of officers shouting orders as they poured into the main doors. Their commands echoed through the expo hall, adding to the cacophony of radios crackling and hurried footsteps.

I moved quickly but without panic, slipping into a narrow corridor that led to the side exit. The space was dimly lit, the faint hum of fluorescent lights above casting a sterile glow over the walls. Pushing open the heavy door, I stepped into the cool night air, the sudden change in temperature brushing against my skin like a sharp reminder of the world outside.

As soon as the door clicked shut behind me, I pulled the hat off my head, my fingers gripping the brim tightly for a moment. The fabric, which had served as my shield of anonymity throughout the evening, now felt conspicuous, almost like a neon sign pointing directly at me. I glanced around quickly, my eyes scanning the dimly lit alleyway. Spotting a nearby trash can, I tossed the hat inside without hesitation.

Ahead, the parking lot was a blur of activity. Flashing red and blue lights bathed the scene in a chaotic glow, shadows dancing across the asphalt as officers darted back and forth. Their voices carried on the cool breeze, radios crackling with clipped phrases and updates. Backup had arrived in full force, turning the once-empty lot into a hive of movement and sound. I caught sight of Gretchen and Pauline.

Their animated gestures and excited chatter suggested they were still caught up in the thrill of whatever they thought had happened. I smoothed my hair, and wiped the sweat from my forehead. My stride was purposeful but measured as I approached them, willing my expression to remain calm and neutral.

Pauline was the first to notice me, her face lighting up with recognition before quickly shifting to concern. "Barbara! Are you okay?" she called out, her voice tinged with alarm. Reaching for my arm, her eyes darted over me, scanning for any signs of injury. "We were worried sick!"

I forced a faint smile, shaking my head as though amused by her concern. "I'm fine," I said lightly, my tone carrying just the right touch of reassurance. "What's going on here?"

"There was a fight!" Gretchen exclaimed, her walker squeaking rhythmically as she moved closer. Her face was alight with excitement, her voice carrying the kind of energy that only a firsthand witness to drama could muster. "A robber tried to run, and someone else in black tackled him right near the doors! It was incredible!"

I widened my eyes in mock surprise, letting a hint of curiosity creep into my expression. "I saw the sirens when I came out," I said, glancing toward the swirling lights of the police cars for emphasis. "I must have taken the wrong exit—I thought I'd find you in the parking lot first."

"You missed the whole thing?" Pauline asked,

her worry softening into a mixture of disbelief and relief. "Well, it's a good thing you didn't get caught up in it!"

"This place is like a labyrinth," I replied with a faint laugh, shaking my head. "I ended up on the wrong side of the building and had to double back."

"Well, you missed a show," Gretchen said. "Someone really gave that robber a dressing down. He didn't stand a chance!"

Her words hung in the air as the sounds of the chaotic parking lot swirled around us. Pauline's worry gave way to chatter, and Gretchen's excitement bubbled over as she recounted every detail of what she'd seen. I nodded along, keeping my responses brief and my tone light, all the while calculating my next move. The scene in the parking lot might have been alive with chaos, but I needed to ensure my exit remained as unremarkable as possible.

Pauline dug into her purse with the kind of determination that suggested she was about to unveil something of utmost importance. When she pulled out her phone, she held it aloft like someone presenting a key piece of evidence in a courtroom. "I got it on video!" she declared triumphantly, her voice filled with excitement as she tapped the screen and turned it toward me.

I forced myself to keep my composure, even as my heart skipped a beat. The grainy footage filled the small screen, chaotic and unfocused, the dim lighting rendering most details indistinguishable. Still, I recognized the scene instantly: the operative near the doors, my own figure lunging forward, and the frantic scuffle that had ended with him tied down. The hat obscured my face just enough to maintain my anonymity, but the proximity of the shot made my pulse quicken. My face might have been hidden, but the figure in black was unmistakably me.

"Look at that!" Pauline continued, her enthusiasm undiminished as she tapped the screen to replay the moment. "You can see the person in black —it's like something out of a movie! They just tackled him like a pro and tied him up like it was nothing!"

"I wish I'd seen it in real life," I said lightly, keeping my tone neutral as I handed her phone back with a smile. "But it's probably better that I didn't get in the way. With my luck, I'd have tripped and made things worse."

Pauline chuckled, tucking the phone back into

her bag with a thoughtful expression. Her brow furrowed slightly, as though she were puzzling out the identity of the mystery figure. "You think it could've been one of the security guards? They were all over the place earlier."

Gretchen snorted audibly, folding her arms over the top of her walker. "Security guards? Please. Did you see how fast that person moved? None of the guards at this place looked like they could chase down a toddler, let alone tackle someone like that."

"She has a point," Pauline admitted with a small shrug. "The ones I saw were mostly standing around checking badges and chatting with each other. They didn't seem like the superhero type."

I raised an eyebrow, feigning mild amusement as I weighed in. "Maybe one of them was more athletic than they looked. Or they brought in someone new just for the event—someone trained for this kind of thing."

Gretchen shook her head firmly, her expression skeptical. "Doubt it. This is Cheerville. If they brought in someone like that, we'd know about it. They'd stick out like a sore thumb, and you know how this town loves its gossip."

"What about one of the officers?" I suggested,

tilting my head as though considering the idea. "Grimal brought in backup, didn't he?"

Pauline let out a laugh, shaking her head. "Oh, I know all the officers in town. I don't think so. None of them are exactly action-movie material, if you know what I mean."

"Could've been a visitor," I mused, keeping my voice casual. "Maybe someone who saw something suspicious and decided to step in."

"A visitor?" Gretchen repeated, her tone skeptical, though less dismissive than before. "That's more likely, I guess."

"It could happen," Pauline said thoughtfully, her expression softening as she considered the idea. "You never know who might be passing through. And sometimes people don't even think about getting involved—it's just instinct, you know?"

I nodded, letting the suggestion settle in their minds. "Whoever it was, they did a good job," I said, my tone firm enough to steer the conversation toward a satisfying conclusion. "Maybe we should ask Grimal tomorrow—he's bound to know more."

"But for now," I added, my voice light and tinged with humor, "why don't we focus on getting home? It's been a long night, and I think we've all had enough excitement for one day."

Pauline glanced at her watch, her eyes widening slightly in surprise. "Goodness, you're right. Let's get out of here before we find ourselves caught up in another adventure."

Gretchen chuckled, her walker squeaking faintly as she turned it toward the car. "I could use some hot tea after all this," she said, her voice carrying a note of exaggerated weariness. "And maybe a piece of chocolate. Or two."

As I walked them to Pauline's car, the two of them continued to speculate, their theories growing increasingly imaginative. One moment it was a tourist with martial arts training; the next, an off-duty firefighter with a secret life as a vigilante. By the time they'd reached their more outlandish ideas—an ex-Navy SEAL who just happened to be passing through town—I was struggling to keep a straight face. I nodded along, adding the occasional comment to keep them engaged while carefully steering the conversation away from anything too close to the truth.

When they were finally settled into the car and Pauline had driven off, I allowed myself a moment to exhale. The parking lot was quieter now, the flashing lights of the police cars still illuminating the scene but no longer accompanied by the same frenetic energy. As I slid into my own car and pulled out of the lot, the chaos faded into the distance. The flashing red and blue lights grew smaller in the rearview mirror, replaced by the stillness of the road ahead.

For now, I had successfully dodged suspicion. The night had been close, too close, but I'd managed to stay one step ahead. As the cool night air seeped in through the cracked window, I allowed myself a brief smile.

ELEVEN

Cheerville hadn't buzzed this much since the Great Pancake Festival Fire of 2007—a disaster that still sparked lively debates at the local diner. Overnight, the town was alight with speculation, and the tech expo hero had become everyone's favorite mystery. Every corner of Cheerville seemed abuzz with chatter. At the grocery store, in the café, and even during senior yoga, snippets of conversation centered around the unknown figure who had tackled a man in black at the LuxTech booth.

Pauline's and Gretchen's social media posts, sprinkled with exclamation marks and custom hashtags, had only fanned the flames of curiosity. Speculation ran wild. Some townsfolk floated plausible theories about undercover agents working to dismantle a criminal network, while others embraced far-fetched ideas involving vigilante hackers or even extraterrestrial intervention. Theories multiplied faster than they could be debunked, each one stranger than the last.

The headline "Cartel's Plot Thwarted in Cheerville: Mystery Hero Saves the Day" or something similar blared across every news site I checked, plastered alongside stock photos of the expo hall. The story wasn't confined to Cheerville anymore; it was everywhere. News anchors dissected the details on national television, and online forums brimmed with conspiracy theories. LuxTech, once a darling of the tech industry, had seen its carefully crafted reputation crumble overnight. Whistleblowers, emboldened by the chaos, had come forward, and investigative journalists quickly connected the dots, exposing the company's shady partnership with a mysterious cartel.

The revelations confirmed what I already knew. Bryce Thornton's death hadn't been a tragic accident, as the initial reports had suggested. It had been deliberate—the first grim test of their weaponized smartwatch technology. Cheerville had been next in line for mass deployment, the small town unwittingly serving as a proving ground for something far more sinister.

But while the cartel's involvement dominated headlines, the story refused to stay focused on the criminal network alone. Thanks to Pauline and Gretchen's fuzzy video, the vigilante theory had taken on a life of its own. The clip, now making the rounds on every major platform, showed a blurry figure in black tackling a man near the expo's front doors. The footage was shaky, chaotic, and grainy, the poor quality obscuring enough details to make identification impossible. Yet that didn't stop the internet from running wild with it.

The headline accompanying the video, "Cheerville's Real-Life Super Spy?" was bad enough. But the hashtag #CheervilleHero had taken off in ways I found both amusing and concerning. Every corner of social media was ablaze with commentary, memes, and artistic renderings of what the "hero" might look like. One post featured a dramatic sketch of a caped figure standing atop a building with Cheerville's skyline in the background, a far cry from the reality of me wrestling an operative with fitness tubing.

Curiosity got the better of me, and I went on Instagram to check the damage. Dandelion stretched lazily across my lap, her small body warm and content as her tail flicked against my arm. Her green eyes half-closed, she let out a soft purr as if she, too, was curious about the internet's latest obsession. My fingers scrolled through a cascade of posts, each more absurd than the last. One particularly dramatic video compilation had paired the blurry footage with an action-movie soundtrack, while another edited in explosions for added flair.

The comments ranged from the outright ridiculous—"Maybe it's a time traveler!" one user suggested with a series of fire emojis—to the eerily perceptive: "They were too efficient. Definitely trained in something," another wrote, earning dozens of likes. Dandelion let out an approving trill as I scrolled past a post featuring yet another snippet of a news article speculating about the mystery hero's identity.

"At least they're creative," I muttered, scratching her ears absently. Her purring deepened in response, a steady rhythm that was oddly grounding amidst the chaos.

Cheerville had always thrived on gossip, but this was on an entirely new level. The town seemed electrified, every conversation charged with the latest developments and rumors. The group chat was now ablaze with theories and speculation:

Pauline:

"I told you it was a vigilante! Did you see how fast they moved? That's not normal for a regular person."

Gretchen:

"Super fast. Definitely not from around here. And it couldn't have been one of our cops either— not with their fitness levels. No offense, but have you seen Chief Grimal try to jog?"

Nancy:

"It has to be someone young, though. Do you think they'll come forward? Maybe someone's already gone to the police."

Agnes:

"Not if they're smart. Someone like that knows how to stay in the shadows. Heroes don't always need credit. Real heroes don't do it for the fame."

I chuckled softly, shaking my head as I read their enthusiastic messages. Dandelion perched beside me on the couch, her tail flicking lazily as though she, too, found the exchange amusing. "Heroes don't always need credit," I echoed under my breath, scratching behind her ears. "Wise words, Agnes. Very wise."

As the chat continued to buzz, Gretchen dropped a link to a video from last night's local news segment, which I'd somehow managed to miss. Curious, I tapped on the link, the screen filling with the familiar logo of Cheerville's evening news. The video opened with dramatic music and a montage of flashing police lights, setting the stage for the breaking story.

The segment featured interviews with police officers and several event attendees who had witnessed the scene firsthand. Chief Grimal, looking particularly gruff and uncomfortable under the camera's scrutiny, stood front and center, his arms crossed and his usual scowl etched deeply into his face. He dismissed the reporter's questions about the so-called vigilante with visible irritation, though his tone remained measured.

The reporter, undeterred, pressed on, her microphone angled toward Chief Grimal with relentless determination. Her expression was sharp, her questions designed to dig into every available angle. "Chief, can you confirm reports that a member of the cartel has been apprehended? And what about the rumored vigilante?" she asked, her voice steady but tinged with excitement.

Grimal's expression darkened, the lines on his

face deepening as he adjusted his stance, his shoulders stiff. "Yes, we've taken a suspect into custody," he said firmly. "We believe this individual has ties to the cartel responsible for recent criminal activity. However, let me be clear: this is far from over. The cartel remains at large, and our investigation is ongoing."

The reporter's eyes lit up at the confirmation, her demeanor shifting as she honed in on the next question. "So, the threat isn't completely neutralized?" she asked, her tone both serious and probing.

Grimal shook his head, his jaw tightening further. "No," he admitted, though his voice remained steady. "But we've disrupted their plans significantly. Their operation involving LuxTech's technology has been stopped. The smartwatches are no longer a danger to the public, and we're working with federal agencies to track down the higher-ups."

The reporter leaned in slightly, her tone turning sharper as she zeroed in on the more tantalizing angle. "And what about the vigilante? The person seen in the footage who seemingly intervened during the chaos at the expo? Are they connected to law enforcement, or is this someone acting independently?"

Grimal's irritation was evident now, his jaw

tightening as he exhaled through his nose. "We have no information on any so-called 'vigilante,'" he replied curtly. His words were deliberate, each syllable clipped. "As far as we're concerned, this was a collaborative effort between law enforcement and event security. That's all there is to say on the matter."

I rolled my eyes as the segment cut to the newscasters in the studio, their expressions a mix of curiosity and excitement. The blurry footage from the expo played in a loop on the screen behind them, the shaky, grainy video analyzed from every angle. One of the anchors leaned forward, her voice brimming with enthusiasm as she declared, "Cheerville's very own Batman? Could the vigilante in black be a local hero? Or is this someone just passing through?"

Her co-anchor chuckled, adding, "Whoever they are, they've certainly captured everyone's imagination. Look at social media—it's going wild! The hashtag #CheervilleHero is trending nationwide."

The video transitioned to a montage of posts from Instagram and Twitter, each one speculating about the identity of the mysterious figure. Some featured amateur sketches, others paired the blurry footage with dramatic music or superhero-style commentary. One particularly creative post had edited the footage to include comic-book-style graphics, complete with "Pow!" and "Bam!" effects as the operative was tackled.

Dandelion gave an approving trill as I turned off the video, her green eyes fixed on me with an expression that almost seemed knowing. "Even you're enjoying this circus, huh?" I murmured, scratching her chin. She responded with a purr, her tail flicking contentedly as if to say, *What's not to enjoy?*

The truth was, the chaos wasn't entirely unwelcome. As long as the speculation stayed focused on a nameless, faceless hero, my role in the takedown would remain a secret. The town could have its fun with theories and wild guesses, but I couldn't afford to let my guard down—not yet.

The doorbell rang, pulling me from my thoughts. I stood, wincing slightly as my hand protested, and made my way to the door. Opening it, I found Octavian standing there, holding a bag of takeout and wearing his usual easy smile.

"Lunch delivery," he said, stepping inside without waiting for an invitation. "I figured you'd be too caught up in the news to cook anything."

"You're a saint," I replied, stepping aside to let

him in. Dandelion leapt down from the desk, her tail flicking as she padded over to investigate.

Octavian set the bag on the kitchen table, taking out delicious ham sandwiches and mushroom soup.

"So," he began, his tone light but teasing, "what do you make of all this?"

"All what?" I asked innocently, pouring water into two glasses.

"This," he said, gesturing to the screen. "Mysterious cartels, tech gone rogue, and some shadowy hero saving the day."

I chuckled. "It's definitely stirred things up. Makes you wonder what kind of person would risk all that."

"A very brave one," he said, his eyes narrowing slightly. "Or a reckless one."

"Probably both," I replied. "But whoever they are, they've given the town plenty to talk about."

As we unpacked the takeout, Octavian's gaze drifted to my left hand, which I'd been flexing absentmindedly. The knuckles were red and slightly swollen—a souvenir from my scuffle at the expo.

"What happened to your hand?" he asked casually, though his tone carried a note of suspicion.

I glanced down, quickly tucking my left hand

under the table. "Oh, pain from old age," I said breezily. "You know how it is—joints acting up, a little too much gardening, that sort of thing."

His lips twitched in amusement, but his eyes remained sharp. "I didn't know gardening could be that dangerous."

He passed me the soup container, his smile lingering as though he wanted to say more but decided against it.

"You know," he said thoughtfully, "sometimes you remind me of Dandelion. Quiet, unassuming… but always up to something."

I laughed, scratching the cat's head as she jumped onto my lap. "Dandelion's a troublemaker," I said. "I'm just a harmless grandmother."

"Harmless," he repeated, his tone laced with doubt. "Right."

After Octavian cleared the table and packed up the leftovers, the doorbell rang again. This time, it was Martin, his lanky frame filling the doorway as he grinned at me.

"Hey, Grandma!" he said, stepping inside. His eyes widened slightly when he spotted Octavian lingering by the kitchen counter. "Oh… uh, hi, Mr. Octavian."

Octavian chuckled. "Just Octavian is fine, Martin. Nice to see you."

Martin nodded awkwardly before turning back to me.

"We were just about the have ice cream," I said. "Want some?"

"Sure." Martin's initial hesitation evaporated as he plopped onto a chair at the kitchen table, his enthusiasm bubbling to the surface. "The vigilante stuff! Have you seen the news? Everyone at school's talking about it!"

"It's hard to miss," Octavian said, joining us at the table with spoons and three empty bowls. He set them down with his usual precision, his gaze flicking toward me as though he were still trying to puzzle something out. My left hand, tucked carefully under the edge of the table, throbbed faintly, but I kept my expression neutral.

"They think whoever it was stopped the cartel from doing something crazy," Martin said, his voice full of excitement as he leaned forward, his elbows on the table. "Like, Bryce's death, the smartwatches, all of it—it's wild!"

I grabbed the chocolate ice cream from the freezer, placing it in the center of the table with a small smile. "A lot of excitement for a small town," I said lightly, handing Martin the scooper.

Martin took it eagerly, filling the bowls with uneven but generous scoops. "You don't think it's someone from Cheerville, do you?" he asked, his tone equal parts curious and conspiratorial. "I mean, they're calling them the Cheerville Hero, but what if it's, like, an actual spy or something?"

Octavian chuckled softly, reaching for his bowl. "A spy in Cheerville? That's a bit far-fetched, don't you think?"

Martin's eyes sparkled with enthusiasm. "Why not? Bryce was into some big tech stuff, right? And then there's this whole cartel connection. It wouldn't be that weird for a spy to show up if something huge was going down."

I hid my amusement behind a bite of ice cream, letting the two of them carry the conversation. "A spy, huh? What do you think they'd look like?" I asked casually, keeping my tone light.

Martin furrowed his brow, clearly giving the question serious thought. "I dunno... maybe someone who's super fit, but not obvious about it. Like, they blend in, you know? And they'd have to be smart— like, crazy smart—to figure out all that tech stuff."

"Hmm," I murmured, swirling my spoon through my ice cream. "That does sound impressive."

"Do you think they'll ever come forward?" Martin pressed, leaning closer. "I mean, if I did something that cool, I'd want people to know."

Octavian shot me a sidelong glance, his lips twitching with suppressed amusement. "Sometimes the best work is done quietly."

Martin shrugged, clearly unconvinced. "Still, it'd be awesome to know who it was. Imagine the stories they could tell!"

As the conversation continued, I let myself relax, savoring the cool sweetness of the ice cream and the warmth of the company. Octavian, ever observant, didn't press me about my hand, though I caught him glancing at it once or twice. Martin's enthusiasm was contagious, filling the room with a sense of energy and possibility.

"Whoever it was," Martin said finally, scooping up the last bit of his dessert, "they saved the day. They're a total legend. Cheerville's lucky to have them, even if we don't know who they are."

I smiled faintly, the weight of the past few days settling into a quiet sense of satisfaction. "Yes," I said softly, more to myself than anyone else. "Lucky, indeed."

Dandelion leapt onto the table, her tail flicking as she watched us with the regal disinterest only a cat could muster. I reached out to scratch her head, her purring blending with the sound of Martin and Octavian's laughter.

For now, the pieces were where they needed to be. The mystery of the Cheerville Hero could stay just that—a mystery.

ABOUT THE AUTHOR

Harper Lin is a *USA TODAY* bestselling cozy mystery author. When she's not reading or writing mysteries, she loves going to yoga classes, hiking, and baking with her family and friends.

For a complete list of her books by series, visit her website.

www.HarperLin.com